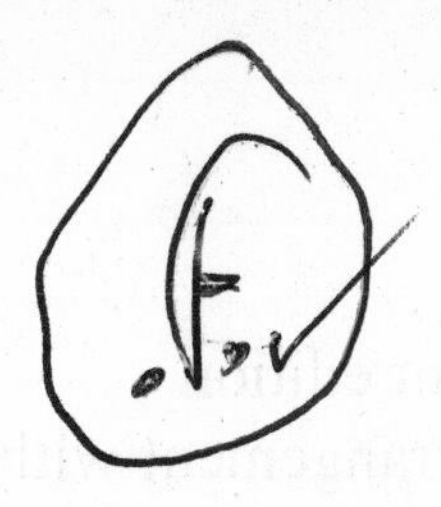

THE DRIFTING KID

WILL ERMINE

CENTER POINT LARGE PRINT
THORNDIKE, MAINE

This Center Point Large Print edition
is published in the year 2019 by arrangement with
Golden West Literary Agency.

Originally published in the US by Doubleday.
Originally published in the UK by Sampson Low.

The text of this Large Print edition is unabridged.
In other aspects, this book may vary
from the original edition.

Set in 16-point Times New Roman type.

ISBN: 978-1-64358-304-4 (hardcover)
ISBN: 978-1-64358-308-2 (paperback)

Library of Congress Cataloging-in-Publication Data

The Library of Congress has cataloged this record
under Library of Congress Control Number: 2019941872

FSC www.fsc.org
resp
FSC
y
vall

THE DRIFTING KID

1

The Kid stepped out of the cabin, a panful of scraps for Trapnell's dog in his hand, and sniffed suspiciously at the raw, earthy tang of melting snow and fresh wet sod stirring with life that filled the morning air.

Here in the high places, where one year's drifts seldom completely disappeared before the early storms of the succeeding fall came to bedeck them with fresh garments of white, the passes were still blocked. But in every direction the morning was murmurous with the rising song of unfettered creeks and rivulets.

The Kid glanced below, where the Big Medicines fell away to gentle valleys and pleasant upland meadows. With a twinge he saw that the grass was green already up to the very edge of the retreating snow patches.

His puny body stiffened as he discovered long lines of brown specks moving slowly across that bright carpet of new grass. At a glance he recognized those moving specks for what they were.

"Elk," he muttered, regret touching his thin face.

For a week now spring had been rolling up these hills to this wild tangle of canyons and spruce-choked draws that lay in the shadows of the Sundance Peaks. Dreading its coming, he had tried to blind himself to its approach. Here was evidence, however, that brooked no denial. Wise in the ways of his world, he knew when the elk herds that had wintered safely in the sheltered basins of the Big Medicines began moving back toward the Great Divide it was the beginning of the season of the Calving Moon for the antlered tribes.

"I guess that settles it!" he grumbled, his narrow shoulders drooping dejectedly with his acceptance of the inevitable. "We won't be here long now!"

A belated storm often struck this mountain country, raging for a day or two with midwinter violence, scattered stock drifting helplessly before it. The Kid knew well enough that no other reason was holding Flat Iron's men at this line camp. A week—two weeks at most—and the danger of a spring blizzard would be past. Any day, then, someone would ride up from the ranch with word that would close the camp until November came again.

The Drifting Kid was only the cook's swamper here at Camp Number 3. When he had caught on, the previous fall, his possessions had been limited to the castoff rags in which he stood and a battered old saddle that he had been lugging around for several years. He was not much better off now, but he liked to tell himself he had never been so happy anywhere. And he was taking into account the cuffings and abuse of Joe Trapnell, Flat Iron's snarling straw boss, and the long, bitter trips down to the ranch for supplies, which he made every third week, no matter what the weather.

For half his life—he was almost sixteen now—he had been doing the odd jobs and dirty work of this short-grass country, jobs at which men turned up their noses; moving on as the seasons changed, with hardly ever a dollar to his name; a gangling, undernourished boy with an unruly mop of yellow hair and a pair of pale blue eyes that managed to conceal their loneliness and the cunning that adversity had built up in him.

Counting the Kid, there were six men at Camp Number 3: Trapnell, the straw boss, three riders, and Big Elmer, the cook. When Trapnell led them up in November, they numbered only four. Late in December, to the surprise of all and the chagrin of Joe Trapnell, the Flat Iron office sent Grady Roberts up to join them. And with his coming life at Camp Number 3 had suddenly become charged with a brooding tension.

Grady Roberts wasn't a Flat Iron man. For the past two years he had worked for the Wyoming Cattle Company, and before that for other big outfits. He was rated a top hand who could catch on anywhere and command the best money on the range. It wasn't necessary for him to take a job in a winter line camp, with its always uncomfortable and often grueling work.

It didn't fool anyone, not even the Kid. He knew the explanation went back to a May evening, year before last, and the slaying of Grady Roberts's friend, Steve Ennis. There had been more than the usual amount of rustling that spring. In the hope of putting it down, Sheriff Hoke Tuller had sworn in several men, Joe Trapnell among them, to assist him and Deputy Sheriff Daggett. According to the story Trapnell and Daggett told when they returned to Medicine Flat, they had been out together and caught Ennis with half a dozen Quarter Moon steers in his possession. Ennis had turned the steers adrift and tried to make a run for it. They had overtaken him up among the lodgepole pines, they said, and called on him to throw down his gun. Instead of obliging, Steve had started blazing away at them, and Trapnell had been compelled to kill him.

The tale had never been believed by men who knew Steve Ennis intimately. His worst known fault was that he gambled away every dollar he got his hands on and was usually hard pressed for money. Not the slightest evidence could be produced, however, that he had turned rustler to get himself a stake.

It was murder, some said, engineered by Trapnell and Chalk Daggett in the hope that it would advance Daggett's ambition to step into old Hoke Tuller's job at the next election. Grady Roberts said nothing, but there was something about his silence that served warning that he wasn't forgetting. It was generally agreed that he was just waiting; that there'd be a break someday and the truth would come out. When that happened, he'd be around to do something about it.

The Kid had heard all the stories. When Grady appeared at Camp Number 3 he was sure the showdown with Trapnell was imminent. Big Elmer and the men shared his feelings. But all were mistaken; Grady took his orders from Trapnell, and when they addressed each other it was only about the work. But there was a wall of ice between them, and Joe Trapnell's studied attempt to ignore it deceived no one.

The weeks and then the months had run together, with Grady saying nothing; just waiting with endless patience. Trapnell's savage temper had taken on an even sharper edge, and his fits of irritation and sullenness became harder to live with. Almost daily of late he had been embroiled with the men, and usually without justification. The Kid had felt his ire too. But never once had Grady raised his voice against him. His silence and restraint seemed to goad Trapnell into new spasms of fury.

Only yesterday the Kid had heard Dutch Krumbine, a Flat Iron veteran, telling Big Elmer that Trapnell was cracking. "Somethin's got to give, Elmer. You can put just so much water behind a dam, and then she lets go."

If the explosion came, the Kid didn't want to miss it. He wasn't in any doubt as to the outcome. His confidence in Grady was a thing apart from the hatred he bore Joe Trapnell. Young as he was, he was a keen judge of men, and tall, softly spoken Grady Roberts, with his sober gray eyes and generous mouth, had not only won from him an idolatrous devotion but provided him with a model on which to pattern his own life.

It was a closely guarded secret with the Kid. It had to be that way because Grady seldom noticed him. The Kid was almost as cautious and secretive in his friendship with Big Elmer. But that was a different sort of friendship. With Elmer he could be a man; with Grady he was just a boy. But they were his friends, and that made everything all right with the Kid. Along the rocky way he had traveled, friends had been few and far between. It put an ache in his heart just to think of parting with Grady and Elmer. There wasn't anything he could do about holding onto Grady. But the Kid had been making plans, and if they worked out, Elmer and he would be together for a long time.

He glanced across the flat to the corral in time to

see Grady riding away. Trapnell's dog, knowing his breakfast was waiting, was charging savagely at the end of its heavy chain and flinging itself into the air, its long, slavering jaws snapping shut with the click of a steel trap as the force of its own rushes jerked it flat. Those gleaming wet fangs were powerful enough to hamstring a full-grown steer or rip a man to ribbons.

The Kid hated that big yellow-eyed beast. So did the men. Trapnell boasted that the animal was more than half wolf. He was going to make a stock dog of him, he said.

"Stock dog!" the Kid muttered contemptuously, the thought rankling in him every time he fed the brute. "I could tell him better. You can't make a heeler out of a dog with that much wolf in him. He'll pull down the first horse or cow Trapnell sends him after."

The door opened behind the Kid and Johnnie Hines stepped out, his saddle tossed over his shoulder. The Kid had put the pan of scraps on the ground and was cautiously shoving it toward the dog with a willow pole.

"You want to watch yourself, Kid," Johnnie advised. "Don't forgit what that yaller-eyed devil did to me." He lowered his voice guardedly. "I'll kill him if he ever makes another grab at me! Trapnell won't stop me!"

The Kid nodded. But Johnnie wasn't fooling him; no one was going to kill Trapnell's dog, unless it was Grady. Johnnie and the other men knew Joe had used his gun on Steve Ennis. They wouldn't cross him.

Johnnie went on to the corral, describing a wide circle that kept him beyond the dog's reach. He and the other men knew to the inch the orbit of freedom the heavy chain allowed the animal.

The big wolf dog eyed him fiercely, its stiff shoulder hair bristling as it devoured the scraps the Kid had brought out. True to its wolf strain, it seldom barked. It did not bark now, but its lips curled back from its dripping fangs in a rasping snarl that was far more menacing than the bark of a dog. It sent a shiver down the Kid's spine.

Unnoticed, Trapnell came around the corner of the long cabin. The Kid still had the pole in his hands and was trying to retrieve the empty pan. Trapnell was instantly enraged.

"Pick up that pan!" he bellowed, his neck muscles swelling until his head seemed several sizes too small for his heavy body. The Kid turned to him appealingly.

"Joe, I'm afraid of him—"

Trapnell kicked the pole out of the Kid's hands. "Pick up that pan as I told you!" He gave the Kid a cuff on the ear that made the latter's head ring. "When you feed my dog, hand the stuff to him!" His face bloodless, the Kid spread his spindling legs and stood his ground, preferring Trapnell's hand to the wolf dog's fangs.

The snarling brute backed up to the post to which it was tethered. The Kid knew this backing up until it had plenty of slack on the chain was the dog's favorite trick. Presently it would hunch its great shoulders and leap in one mighty lunge to the very end of the chain.

Trapnell mistook this backing away for cringing. He knew the dog hated him, and he had good reason to believe it feared him, for he had kicked and beaten it from the day it had come into his possession. Fury boiled over in him, cording his square, rocky face.

Picking up a rock, he hurled it at the dog with vicious force. His aim was accurate. The big wolf dog grunted with pain and momentarily rolled its yellow eyes at Trapnell. But Trapnell and the rock were only annoying interruptions in the game of stalking Johnnie, now halfway down to the corral.

The latter looked back over his shoulder, more interested in Trapnell than in the dog. He didn't like one any better than the other. But he had always walked wide of Joe, and he had kept his distance from the dog until one night in December, when he thoughtlessly took a short cut across the flat. The dog was on him in a flash, ripping his right shoulder almost to the bone. He had beaten off the tawny brute with the barrel of his gun and left it stretched out stiffly in the snow. He knew the dog had never forgotten that beating. What he couldn't understand was why it had attacked him in the first place.

The Kid could have told him. He knew that even as a puppy the dog's strong wolf strain made it suspicious of human scent and that Trapnell's treatment had whipped suspicion into an implacable hatred of all men.

Trapnell ripped out an oath and bent to pick up another rock. As he straightened he saw out of the corner of his eye that Elmer and old Dutch had stepped out. Dutch was content to watch, but Elmer rolled up his soiled apron and stepped in between Trapnell and the Kid. He was an obese man, no longer young, with jowls that sagged as though he had weights in them. From his kitchen window he had seen Joe cuff the boy. His round little eyes were blazing wrathfully in their folds of fat.

"Slappin' him around again, eh?" he wheezed, drawing up his shapeless bulk. "I told you to keep yore hand off him, Joe."

The Kid held his breath. He knew Elmer was over his depth in tangling with Trapnell. Ranch cooks are a hard lot as a rule. Elmer long had had the reputation of being just a little meaner, with a tough walrus hide just a little thicker, than most. The Kid knew it was all bluff, his armor against the hard knocks and loneliness of his life. There wasn't a fighting bone in his all-huge body.

Trapnell grinned evilly. He believed he saw through this man too.

"So what?" he demanded flatly.

His contemptuous grin was instantly erased as he saw Elmer staring past him, eyes and pendulous mouth torn wide in spellbound amazement. It whirled Trapnell around in time to see the big wolf dog lunging through the air at Johnnie. It was three feet off the ground, every ounce of its magnificent strength coordinated in one frenzied plunge.

Even as Trapnell turned, the great beast hit the end of the chain, jerking it so taut that for a fraction of a second it hung in the air rigid as an iron bar. The backlash spun the powerful dog end over end, slamming it on the ground with a shivering thud. As it struck, a link snapped, the report sharp and flat as the cracking of a rifle.

The Kid was the first to find his tongue.

"You better grab him, Joe!" he urged anxiously as the dog reared up on its hunkers, sides heaving.

It flicked a glance at the trailing end of chain and seemed to realize it was free. Shoulder hair poaching, the slavering brute gathered itself to spring, its attention once more focused on Johnnie Hines.

Trapnell, Elmer, and Dutch stood silent, helpless to move or speak.

"Run, Johnnie! Run!" the Kid screeched.

Johnnie stood frozen in his tracks. In another

second the big dog lunged at him. Only a side step at the last split second saved the puncher.

The force of the animal's rush carried it past him, but it no sooner struck the ground than it whirled and came at him again. With all the strength in his wiry body Johnnie hurled his saddle at the charging lobo. It knocked the animal down. Before it had time to hurl itself at him a third time, he whipped out his gun and fired.

The first shot killed the dog, but Johnnie, his nerves badly snarled, stood there and emptied his .44 into the shuddering carcass.

Trapnell went striding across the flat, his step stiff with rage. The Kid and the others followed him.

"Throw down that gun!" he growled at Johnnie.

The latter came out of his abstraction, his face streaked with gray. A rough, tough little bantam, always ready for a fight, he had often said he was not afraid of Trapnell, but now that the chance to stand up to him was his, he knew he had only been whistling in the dark.

"What's eatin' you, Joe?" he cried. "I couldn't let that devil kill me!"

Trapnell hunched his shoulders and brought up his long arms. "Throw down that gun!" he repeated.

Knowing he had to fight, courage came back to Johnnie and, having no rules to bother him, he whipped back his arm and flung his gun at

Trapnell's head with force enough to brain him.

Joe ducked, and the long-barreled .44 sailed harmlessly over his head, carrying away his hat. Sucking in his breath with a noisy rasp, he closed in.

Johnnie was quick. He hit Trapnell three times before the latter threw a long, looping right that jarred the smaller man to his knees. But Johnnie kept on moving, made Trapnell miss two or three times, and with his head clearing stung him repeatedly.

Trapnell took everything that was thrown at him and continued to wade in. The Kid groaned to himself; it was plain to him that Johnnie couldn't hurt the big man. He glanced at Elmer and Dutch, wondering if they realized how the fight must end. He found their faces strained with excitement. They spoke no word, but their sympathies were all against Trapnell.

Though Joe was just a rough-and-tumble fighter, he could throw a punch without setting himself for it. He proved it a moment later. Johnnie stepped in. Before he could get away Trapnell threw that long, looping right again. It lifted Johnnie to his toes, and this time Trapnell followed it up with a bone-crunching hook that closed the little man's left eye.

The pace slowed. Trapnell had things his own way now. Methodically he started to cut his man down, an inch at a time. Johnnie was soon helpless. Trapnell could have finished him with a blow. But that was not his way. Every groan he wrung from Johnnie was wine to his sadistic impulses.

The Kid stole another glance at Elmer. Elmer's sagging jowls were pasty. He winced every time Trapnell's fist crashed into Johnnie Hines's battered face. A thought was mirrored in Elmer's eyes. The Kid read it correctly and was glad it wasn't Elmer who was taking this beating.

Johnnie went to his knees. He got up slowly. Joe waited for him to rise, then knocked him down again.

The fight should have been stopped. But no one said a word. Later they would talk about it and damn Trapnell.

Old Dutch had seen enough. He turned away and limped over to the barn. A horse had fallen on him earlier in the week.

Trapnell continued to cut Johnnie's face to ribbons.

The Kid tugged at Elmer's arm and tried to drag him away. The big man shook him off; a spell had been put on him. Wanting to leave, he could not tear himself away.

For minutes, only the deep breathing of the fighters and the thudding of Trapnell's fists broke the silence that lay thick and heavy on the morning air.

Terror had begun to grip the Kid. He knew

there was nothing he could do to end the fight. If only Grady were there, he thought. "Grady would stop it," he told himself.

A sound registered on his ears that had not been there before. It was unmistakable—the clip-clop of a running horse.

The Kid's heart leaped as he saw a rider flash into view and realized it was Grady.

"He heard the shots and turned back!" he muttered.

Roberts rode across the flat and reined in a few feet from Trapnell. He didn't get down from the saddle; he just sat there waiting, silent, his gray eyes cold and accusing.

Johnnie was down again. He got up slowly. Trapnell's fist flashed back, but he didn't let it fly. Something pulled his eyes to the man on horseback, and he let his hand fall. It was as though a will stronger than his own had taken charge of him.

"The dirty little skunk killed my dog, Roberts! I ain't standin' for it!"

Grady nodded. He knew Trapnell had no feeling for the dog; his rights had been invaded; that's what he was avenging. His reaction would have been the same had someone broken one of his ropes or put a nick in his razor.

"You git your roll and go below," Trapnell growled at Johnnie. "Corson will have your time for you when you git to the house."

Johnnie picked up his empty gun. "I'll square this with you someday, Trapnell, unless somebody beats me to it," he muttered painfully.

He shuffled off toward the cabin. The Kid and Big Elmer stood there. Trapnell glared at them. "You got work inside, the two of you! Git movin'!"

He had nothing to say to Roberts. The Kid found it significant, coming on top of the fact that he had deemed it necessary to give Grady an explanation.

"Just a minute, Trapnell," Grady said in his quiet way as Joe started for the corral.

"Wal?" the latter growled.

"I wouldn't get too excited over the killing of a dog, Trapnell. It's a little different when a man has his best friend knocked off. That's all I had to say."

He wheeled his bronc and rode away. Trapnell, understanding him perfectly, continued on to the corral.

"Guess that was tellin' him where he gits off," the Kid declared, glancing up at Big Elmer. "But don't you have no run-ins with him on my account, Elmer; you leave him to Grady. You understand?"

Elmer nodded woodenly. "I won't have no run-ins with him."

2

They found Johnnie Hines sitting on his bunk, shoving cartridges in his gun. He set the trigger on an empty chamber and slipped the .44 into the holster.

"Kid, you won't have to feed that dog no more," he muttered. "I wisht I'd saved a slug for Trapnell. He'd shore have got it!"

The Kid nodded woodenly. "You better forget the gun, Johnnie. There's other ways of squarin' this."

"What? Waitin' around and doin' nothin' like Roberts? Not for me! Joe Trapnell wants to git in my way just once!"

The Kid and Elmer took him into the kitchen and washed the blood from his face. Johnnie's right eye was badly puffed. Elmer offered to cut a piece of raw beef for it.

"Don't bother," Johnnie told him. "I'll keep a little snow on it on the way down."

He gathered up his belongings and rolled them in his blankets. He had been gone an hour when Trapnell rode up to the cabin and stalked into the kitchen for a cup of coffee.

"Where's Dutch?" he demanded.

"The barn," the Kid told him.

"You tell him I said to jerk the pelt off the dog and toss the carcass over the cliff." Over the rim of his cup he gave the Kid and Big Elmer a searching, hostile glance and was disappointed not to find some further evidence of rebellion against his rule. "Hines got what was comin' to him. If anybody else around here is nursin' any grudge, they can be taken care of too."

He stormed out, saying he was going to ride the rim to the east.

"Humph!" the Kid snorted contemptuously as Trapnell rode away. "Shootin' his mouth off to us, but he sings another tune to Grady. Goin' to have himself made a pair of mittens out of that pelt, I reckon. That's the kind of a stinker he is!"

The Kid went down to the barn and communicated Trapnell's order to Dutch. The latter was fashioning some new boards for the corral gate. He put down his tools carefully.

"So that's what he wants, eh?"

Dutch shook his head disgustedly. But he was a prudent man and kept his thoughts largely to himself. It enabled him to live within an inch of danger without ever becoming directly involved. In a way it explained why he had let the Kid go on believing that their paths had never crossed until a few months ago. Actually Dutch had first seen him years ago, a ragged, forlorn bit of humanity perched on the top rail of Lafe Stringer's horse corral at Cain Springs, even then a fading, down-at-the-heel stage station on the old Pitchstone Road. The boy was called Davy in those days, and Lafe Stringer was his father. Death had taken the lad's mother when he was only three or four. Men who knew said that hard work and Lafe's shiftlessness had killed her.

Old Dutch liked the Kid. For the start he had, Dutch thought the boy had turned out better than might have been expected.

"Why don't you tell Trapnell to go chase himself and pull his own pelt?" the Kid inquired hopefully. "You didn't hire out to do his dirty work."

"No, Davy, I'm too old to tell him to go to hell. I couldn't make it stick. Anyways, he's boss here . . . About time for you to be goin' below, ain't it?"

The Kid nodded and said, "Just about."

"Wal, don't you go airin' your opinions when you git down to the house. Mind yore own business; this ain't yore quarrel. Things allus git settled, give 'em time. This ain't no exception."

"When?" the Kid asked.

Dutch shrugged noncommittally and wouldn't say any more. The Kid wandered back to the kitchen and his chores. Later Dutch walked across the flat and jerked the dog's pelt and hung it on the corral to dry.

If the men came in at noon they sat down to soup, bread, and coffee. Neither Trapnell nor Grady came in today. Dutch, Elmer, and the Kid ate by themselves. No matter what they spoke about, the conversation always got back to Trapnell. Anything they had to say about Johnnie always brought them around to Joe Trapnell. Johnnie had said he'd square his account with Joe. Did Dutch think he would? If Grady Roberts was mentioned, there was Trapnell again. What was Roberts waiting for?

The Kid was outspoken; so was Big Elmer; Dutch was cagey and wouldn't be drawn out. Though he was at some pains to learn exactly what had passed between Trapnell and Grady that morning, he refused to express an opinion as to its significance.

"Dutch, you got a piece of rubber where your backbone ought to be," the Kid protested.

Dutch's faded old eyes flashed reprovingly. "Yo're awful young, Kid. Awful young. When you git to be as old as I be you'll have sense enough to git out of the way when you see a storm comin' that you can't stop."

He usually sat smoking for half an hour. Today he took his pipe down to the barn.

There was an old bench outside the kitchen door. The sun got around to it in the early afternoon. With the dishes washed and preparations for supper completed, the Kid and Elmer came out and sat there for an hour. The day had turned unseasonably warm. Off to the west, where the Tetons were just fuzzy pinches of cotton, thunderheads were piling up.

"Goin' to rain," said the Kid.

"Yeh, goin' to rain all right," Elmer agreed.

With Trapnell away and the dog gone forever, it was peaceful on the little flat. Dutch had moved down to the corral gate. The blows of his hammer echoed pleasantly.

"Nice here when Trapnell ain't around," the Kid observed, his pale blue eyes veiled with some remote thought. Elmer nodded and puffed his short pipe.

The Kid built himself a cigarette. Minutes passed before he said, "We won't be here much longer." His tone was forlorn for all its studied carelessness.

Elmer nodded ponderously; he had the mind of a child; it was the Kid who was the man. "That's what I was thinkin'; we won't be here much longer."

"Suppose they'll keep you on down below for a while?"

"I suppose. Flat Iron always sends a wagon out for the calf brandin'. I cooked with the wagon last spring. It don't last long."

"No job lasts long," the Kid observed bleakly. Eyes on his cigarette, he said, "What'll you be doin' then, Elmer?"

"I dunno," was the weighty answer. "Last fall in the Flat, they said the guv'ment was goin' to build a new highway into the Park this spring. Be some jobs in the cook tent. But I dunno, Kid; I dunno."

The Kid nodded soberly. "That's the way it is with me—I dunno." And then, with enormous gravity, "Summer's the slow time in my line too. But somethin' always turns up," he added, not wanting to give Elmer the impression that he wasn't equal to the situation.

"Yep, sumpin' allus turns up," Elmer agreed after great deliberation.

"But it don't get a man nowheres." The conversation was getting just where the Kid wanted it to be. With great guile he said, "You get a job for a few months, and somethin' happens, or you get fired. Jobs don't put no fat on the cat, Elmer. It ain't like bein' your own boss. When you're your own boss, ain't no one tellin' you where to head in or handin' you your time just when you figger you're all set for a spell. Ain't no one routin' you out of your blankets at four in the mornin' when you'd like to snooze till five. Ain't no messin' around with a crock of flapjack batter, when what you want to be cookin' is ham and eggs. An' all the time you're layin' up a dollar or two for a rainy day."

He stole a cautious glance at Elmer, to see how he was taking it. Elmer, seemingly impressed, was nodding to himself, a rapt expression on his broad face. A feeling of elation began to course through the Kid; he had been leading up to this moment for weeks. He masked it adroitly, and his eyes were suddenly as vacant as an Indian's. With deceiving innocence he said, "I ain't tryin' to tell you what to do, Elmer; I know you wouldn't be interested."

"Hunh!" the big man grunted. "Lot you know, Kid, sayin' that! A fella gits stuck in a rut, but he can't do nuthin' about it. Wantin' ain't all there is to it; you got to git a chance."

"We got a chance, Elmer—you and me," the boy assured him, his voice edged with a pathetic earnestness. "I been thinkin' of it a lot. I'm tellin' you Cain Springs is just waitin' for a couple fellas like us."

This was not the first time the Kid had mentioned Cain Springs to Elmer. For weeks his conversation had been slyly studded with careless references to the abandoned stage station on the Pitchstone Road. Often it was only a word or two, seemingly dropped aimlessly. The Kid had weighed their effect with a shrewdness beyond his years. He had the patience of a good fisherman, and when Elmer nibbled at the bait the Kid dropped the subject and turned to something else, making the big man come to him. If he never said too much nor grew too enthusiastic, it was only because he was moving toward his goal with cunning indirection.

Elmer had been over the Pitchstone Road, the main thoroughfare between Cody and the Clark's Fork country, and he had vague memories of Cain Springs, a green spot in the Sand Hills in those days.

Stockmen and freighters still used the Pitchstone Road, but it swung far south of Cain Springs now, adding a long twelve miles for man and beast. A shifting hill of sand had marched across the old road and doomed the Springs five years back.

"I dunno about Cain Springs, Kid," Elmer declared with a discouraging lack of enthusiasm. "Can't be much left there."

"It's just as it was." The Kid was not insistent; he spoke as one does who states a fact that is not open to dispute. "I told you I drifted in there a couple years ago and looked things over. There wa'n't nothin' changed, 'cept the cottonwood at the side of the house was bigger. The grass around the Springs was as green and pretty as ever." The Kid's tone was unconsciously wistful. "It was all so natural, I figgered the old man would stick his head out the door and yell for me to come runnin'."

Elmer nodded understandingly. The Kid and he had exchanged many confidences through the long winter months, always swearing each other to secrecy.

"Two, three years make a difference," the big man argued. "Mebbe the old station's all gone by now."

"No, she ain't," the Kid declared confidently. "The house and barn can stand some fixin', but they're there. Grady Roberts was in last fall."

"You been talkin' to Roberts?" Elmer demanded, aggrieved. "You told me you wasn't goin' to say nuthin' about the Springs to no one but me."

"Elmer, you take the cake!" the Kid exclaimed. "I didn't tell Grady nothin'. He didn't know what I was gettin' at, askin' him a couple questions. He wouldn't say nothin' if he did."

"All right," the big man muttered. "I was jest wonderin'. I got nuthin' agin Roberts. I reckon yo're smart enough not to let what we got to say to each other git any further. Goin' to take money to fix up the station."

"We don't have to do anythin' about the buildin's right off. It's the road that's goin' to take work."

"Yeh, the road," Elmer echoed. "That's what I mean; the road. You can't make no money runnin' a station if it ain't on a road."

"Gee, Elmer, you can be thick when you want to!" the Kid protested tragically. "Do you think I'd be wastin' my time talkin' about Cain Springs if I didn't see the way to fix that road? Swell chance! We'd have to go at it the way they do in the desert country. String a couple wire fences across the face of that sand hill and lace 'em up with sagebrush. As soon as they fill up, go a little higher and build a couple more. In a year's time we can have the crest of that hill so far back from the old road that the drift will begin runnin' the other way."

The Kid was all business now and forgot his role of studied restraint with Elmer.

"You got a head on you, Kid," the cook acknowledged appreciatively. "I seen that trick worked out in Nevada. How you figgerin' to git rid of the sand that's in the road? Dig it out?"

"Dig out some and brush the rest with sage. We can cut enough in a month. It'll have to be piled on two feet thick. When it gets ground down into the sand the road will have bottom again. Get that done and we'll be all set. Ain't no one goin' to take the long way round when they can save twelve miles by comin' through the Springs. When Lafe had the station he used to charge two bits' toll. We can charge it, too, and folks will be glad to pay."

For a moment he was carried away by his own eloquence. A tremulous smile touched his thin face.

"Gee, I can see it so plain," he murmured. "You doin' the cookin', Elmer, and me tendin' stock and lookin' after things."

The big man cleared his throat. The spell of

the Kid's dream had caught him too. "You shore make it sound good," he declared soberly. "I could go for a place like that—anchored somewheres, no more movin' on. It would suit me fine. Mebbe I could have a little garden—"

"Sure you could! And some chickens. There's a porch on the house, Elmer. We could plant some hop vines—they grow quick—and train 'em up on strings. That would make it nice and shady. In the afternoon I could sluice the porch down with a bucketful of water to cool things off . . . It would be nice, sittin' there, waitin' for some outfit to roll in."

"Hop vines don't have no nice flowers—not like mornin'-glories," Elmer objected. "My ma used to have mornin'-glories climbin' all over the porch."

The Kid had no objection to morning-glories.

"They got scads of 'em around the 7 Bar house," he said. "Missus Button is always savin' seeds. Reckon she'd give me all we needed. With good cookin' and clean beds, we ought to be full up most every night."

"Wouldn't be no complaints about the cookin'," Elmer boasted quietly. "I dunno 'bout keepin' the rooms clean. Mebbe we'd need a woman—"

"No, Elmer," the Kid said flatly. "We don't want no woman around. They always get bossy."

In the Utopia Elmer had often visioned for himself there had always been a woman. But he didn't insist. The Kid had thrown open the doors to a dreamworld of happiness and contentment, and Elmer was not only disinclined to be critical but actually afraid to scrutinize it too closely lest he destroy it completely.

They talked for an hour. The Kid made it all sound so real and easy. Elmer wanted to believe. Only one thing troubled him: how were a man and boy without money to do so much? But gazing at the Kid's eager face, he put even that doubt behind him temporarily.

"Don't let nothin' slip about this to no one," the Kid warned. "Somebody would just like to come along and beat us to it."

"I ain't the talky kind," Elmer averred. "I won't let nuthin' slip. See that you don't—not even to Roberts."

The Kid knew Elmer was jealous of Grady.

"Shucks, we're pardners, ain't we? You don't have to worry about me sayin' anythin' to him."

Without any disloyalty to Elmer, the Kid could have wished it were the other way around: that he and Grady were partners.

A drop of rain touched his face. He brushed it away.

"Gee, I wish we was startin' for Cain Springs tomorrow!"

Tomorrow was too soon for Elmer. With something akin to relief, he thought of the calf branding. He said, "The spring roundup won't be wound up before the first of May. That'll give us plenty of time to think things over."

There was a faint reservation in his tone. The Kid caught it and stiffened instantly.

"What do you mean by that?" he demanded, his voice sharp with suspicion. "We're all set, ain't we?"

"Shore, Kid, shore," Elmer protested, trying hard to dissemble his confusion. The Kid was a smart one, he thought. "I was jest thinkin', a lot of things can happen in four, five weeks. We gotta make plans too."

"We got to make plans all right," the Kid grumbled, not wholly mollified. "Four, five weeks will pass quick. When I get through here I'm goin' to hang around Medicine Flat a day or two till somebody comes in from 7 Bar; I can always catch on there for a spell; Missus Button likes the way I fix things up around the house. We can keep in touch, Elmer."

"Yeh, we shore got to do that," the big man agreed. "If you don't want to go to 7 Bar you come with me on the wagon. I'll get Corson to take you on; you can rustle wood for me."

The Kid's face lit up. "You mean that, Elmer?"

"Shore—"

"Gee, we could be together all the time—talkin' things over and gettin' ready."

"Shore," Elmer mumbled.

It was raining quite hard by now, a thin, fine

rain, with a rising wind behind it. It began to drive into their faces and they went inside.

At the corral old Dutch stuck it out until he had his job finished. Unhurried, he gathered up his tools and limped back to the barn. He had work to do there. He was repairing a bridle when the Kid came in for an armful of wood ten minutes later.

"Whistlin', eh?" Dutch murmured. "Things must be lookin' good, Kid."

"Aw, they're lookin' all right, Dutch," the Kid answered offhandedly. He knew old Dutch had been around in his day and surely knew something about the Pitchstone Road. He would have liked to question him, but caution forbade it. "This is goin' to be a real sod soaker," he said, busy with the wood.

"Yup, it'll rain two, three days," said Dutch. "Goin' to give you a wet trip tonight, Kid."

"Mebbe I won't be goin'," the latter answered surprisingly. "Elmer says he's got flour and canned stuff enough to last a few days."

"Yup," Dutch said, and went on with his work. He was not unaware of the growing bond between Elmer and the Kid. He had never tried to understand it, and he didn't try to understand it now; he only hoped Elmer wouldn't be rash enough to tell Trapnell what to do. It was time for the Kid to go below, and he'd go, come hell or high water. When something had to be done,

Joe got it done. It made him a valuable man and explained why he always had a job.

"What do you mean by sayin' yup?" the Kid demanded.

In a sudden burst of frankness Dutch said, "I mean you better not cross Joe this evenin'. You do what he tells you. And don't you git to figgerin' Grady will be any help to you if you git in a jam. He's playin' his own cards."

"That's what I'm doin'," the Kid flared back without a second's hesitation. "The way things are shapin' up, I can afford to take Trapnell's backwash a few days longer. Reckon it's the last shovin' around I'll have to take."

He gathered up his wood and started to leave.

"What you aimin' to do, Kid?" Dutch inquired with greater interest than he permitted his tone to suggest.

"I ain't sayin'," the boy answered from the doorway. "But I'm lookin' ahead, I can tell you. No more of this driftin' for me!"

3

Evening closed in early, a blanket of fog settling over the hills. Grady Roberts came up from the corral, his saddle and wet riding gear slung over his shoulder. The Kid stepped out from the kitchen.

"Back, eh?" he said. "The goin' was kinda rough, I reckon."

"Not too bad, Kid. It's the last of the snow."

Grady deposited his saddle on a wooden peg and pulled off his slicker. The Kid watched him, so tall and wiry, an air of authority about whatever he did.

Over his shoulder Grady said, "Did Johnnie get away all right?"

"He got away," the Kid answered.

Dutch was reading an old newspaper. He looked up over his glasses, waiting for Grady's comment. It didn't come; the tall man had nothing further to say about Johnnie.

Trapnell stamped in a few minutes later. He asked Roberts about the stock, where it was bunched and how it looked. This was the business they had been hired to perform. Grady told him what he had seen in the course of the day. Business out of the way, conversation between them ended abruptly.

Supper was soon on the table. The wind had gone out of the rain, and as they ate it fell in a steady torrent.

Supper over, Trapnell pulled off his boots and sat by the stove, busy with a pencil and a tally book in which he kept a record of his stewardship of Camp Number 3. His report made out, he tore a couple of leaves from the book and wrote a letter.

The Kid was in the kitchen washing dishes when Trapnell called him.

"You're due to go below tonight." Trapnell's tone was gruff. He knew Grady and Dutch, playing cribbage, were listening. "See that you git an early start. The crick's risin' and you won't git acrost if you don't."

Elmer looked up from his plate; he was just finishing his supper. "Purty bad night, Joe," he ventured. "I got enough to carry us along for a day or two."

Trapnell reared up in his chair, eyes narrowing with fury.

"Who's givin' orders here?" he jerked out fiercely. "I told the Kid to go."

Roberts and old Dutch sat stiffly silent, and under the pounding of the rain an ominous hush settled over the cabin.

A picture of Johnnie Hines being beaten to a pulp flashed in the Kid's mind and drove the blood from his face.

"Sure, Joe," he said with a mirthless little laugh, trying to pretend there was nothing amiss. "A little rain never hurt no one." He flashed a glance at Elmer, beseeching him to say no more. "You get your list ready, Elmer, and I'll be on my way. If you're worryin' about the flour gettin' wet, forget it! I never spoiled nothin' yet, bringin' it up."

This was pure artistry on the Kid's part. With a smothered sigh of relief he saw Elmer heave himself to his feet and start for the kitchen. To further divert Trapnell's animosity, the Kid said, "What'll I tell the boss, Joe, if he asks any questions about Johnnie?"

"You won't have to tell him nothin'," Trapnell rapped. "I'll give you a letter for the old man."

Roberts and Dutch resumed their game, and the tension was suddenly gone from the room. With studied carelessness the Kid gathered up Elmer's cup and plate and carried them to the kitchen.

"Gee, Elmer, I'm glad you didn't say no more," he got out tensely, his voice lowered against being overheard in the other room. "With only a few weeks to go, we don't want no trouble with him."

"The dirty rat!" Elmer muttered. "Somebody ought to stop him!"

"Yeh, I know—and somebody will. Just give us a couple months and we'll show him who he was pushin' around. But get this straight: Joe Trapnell don't mean anythin' to us."

Elmer was silent for a moment or two.

"I guess you're right," he agreed at last, anger running out of him. "I guess that's the way to look at it."

On his trips below the Kid left one evening and was back the next. Four miles of steep downhill trail brought him to a barn on Emigrant Creek. Flat Iron kept a wagon there. Putting his mount and a pack animal into harness, he drove the rest of the way to the house, following the twin ruts that were charitably called a road.

With Elmer's list and Trapnell's letter stowed away in his pocket, he picked up his saddle and went down to the corral. The night was as black as it was wet, the footing treacherous, but he knew the way, and when he reached the creek it was not yet nine o'clock. As Trapnell had warned, Emigrant Creek was running high. He harnessed the horses and drove across without difficulty.

When he reached Flat Iron's home ranch, he put up the horses and headed for the bunkhouse. Late as it was, the men piled out of their blankets and surrounded him. Here was an eyewitness, fresh from the scene of hostilities, and they wanted the details of the big fight.

The Kid tried to dodge their questions. He

couldn't deny there had been a fight, but he pretended to know very little about it.

"Don't try to come that on us!" Bill Spane, Johnnie's friend, told him. "I talked to Johnnie. You know all about it. The fight started over Trapnell's dog, didn't it?"

"I guess it did," the Kid had to admit.

They dragged the story out of him but failed to maneuver him into siding against Trapnell.

"What the hell is wrong with Roberts?" someone questioned. "Has he lost his nerve? I figgered he was goin' to ram a gun down that skunk's throat."

"That's what I want to know," said Bill Spane. "What'd he go up there for if it wasn't to put the crawl on Trapnell? Looks like Grady's pullin' in his horns."

It needled the Kid into an unguarded outburst.

"You fellas make me sick!" he whipped out contemptuously. "Grady knows what he's doin'. He's cuttin' his man down an inch at a time. That's the way it hurts most."

The crew tried to enlarge on this opening, but the Kid withdrew into his shell and Spane and the other men had to let him go.

He saw Reb Corson, Flat Iron's foreman, in the morning, expecting another grilling. Corson read Trapnell's letter, crumpled it into a ball, and tossed it in the fire. He didn't have a question to ask. Cowboy fights were an old story with him.

If the work got done, he wasn't interested in the fights.

The rain had not slacked off for a second. Up in the high places the melting snow was pouring an icy flood into Emigrant Creek. Corson mentioned it.

"Maybe you better not try to go up till tomorrow," he suggested.

"I can get across, Reb," the Kid argued. He had three or four reasons for wanting to be back at Camp Number 3 quickly.

"All right," Corson agreed. "You be careful; I don't want to lose a couple horses. You pull out of here by noon."

The Kid got away a few minutes after dinner. Huddled under a canvas tarp, he took the soggy trail into the hills. Long before he got his first glimpse of the creek he could hear it growling. He found it over its banks, a rushing torrent. It was full of slush ice.

Ordinarily Emigrant Creek could be forded anywhere but at the deep holes. This afternoon, swollen to three times its usual size, it presented a strange appearance. The Kid studied it for some minutes, getting his bearings.

The horses were rolling their nostrils nervously and giving every sign of not wanting to take to the water. To make the crossing easier for them the Kid drove up the creek until he was thirty yards above the spot on the opposite bank where he wanted to come out. By quartering down with the current, the team would have a better chance to hold its feet.

He clucked to the horses, but they refused to budge. When he applied the whip they reared violently and threatened to overturn the wagon. The Kid fought them and straightened them out. Not giving them time to reconsider, he shouted encouragement and urged them ahead. The whip fell heavier and heavier. Suddenly the animals bolted into the icy water and he lashed them across. Ten minutes later he drove into the barn, cold and wet.

"By jeebers, this is the last time I'll be doin' this!" he growled. "I'll show some of these high and mighty gents I ain't mud under their feet!"

He shook the water out of his floppy hat and hung up the piece of canvas under which he had huddled on the seat of the wagon. Water ran from it in little rivulets. After he had unhitched the horses he fed them their supper.

He had two cases of assorted canned vegetables and fruit in the wagon. He split the wooden cases into kindling and built a fire near the open door. Though the old barn was drafty, the fire threw some heat, and he warmed himself.

It was growing dark already. Ahead of him were four tough, uphill miles. Old Bess, the pack mare, was surefooted, but he'd have to let her take her time.

"Be midnight before I hit camp," he grumbled to himself. "I reckon Elmer will be all right till I get there."

He drew some comfort from the thought and got out tobacco and papers and fashioned a cigarette. Things were certainly going to be different once Elmer and he were settled at the Springs. Cain Springs was the only home he had ever known. Though the pickings there had always been very slim for him, the passing years had rubbed out the unpleasant memories and left him only the happy ones that a boy might be expected to retain.

The Kid remembered his mother vaguely. She had yellow hair like his own and his blue eyes. Two summers ago at a gospel tent in Medicine Flat, he had heard a woman sing a song that quickened memories in him. He knew his mother had sung that song. He had heard men say that his father had led her a dog's life. The Kid knew it was true. Even before he was ten he had realized for himself that Lafe Stringer was lazy and worthless. He had been glad to get away from him. Later, when he learned that Lafe had died in Cody, the news, reaching him belatedly, caused him no grief or regret.

By the flickering light of a smoky lantern the Kid pawed over the canned stuff. He knew there would be some cans of peaches. He found one and eyed it hungrily. Sure that he could square himself with Elmer, he produced his pocketknife and punched a hole in the top of the can. When he had finished drinking the juice he widened the hole and ate the peaches.

With a grunt of fullness he tossed the empty can in the brush. The rain was still falling steadily and giving no indication of letting up.

The horses had finished their oats. The Kid put his saddle on the pony and adjusted the panniers on old Bess. One of the panniers, or baskets, was reserved for the sack of flour, carefully wrapped in a waterproof tarp. The fifty-pound sack was too heavy for him to handle easily, so he led the mare to the rear of the wagon and made her stand against the endgate. With a lot of grunting and heaving he got the flour into the basket. Loading the other stuff was easy enough; he just tossed it in.

The fire had burned out. The Kid scattered the ashes and was ready to leave. With the strip of wet canvas drawn over his shoulders and the mare's lead rope in his hand, he rode out into the rain.

With the coming of evening the temperature had dropped a few degrees and a mist was rising from the ground that made the black night even more impenetrable. The best the Kid could do was to depend on the horses to find the trail. They splashed through puddles that he could not see and plowed through mud that was fetlock-deep.

At the end of an hour the steep uphill climb and the heavy going had the horses blowing. The Kid pulled up to rest them. Here the trail skirted a stand of young aspens. The Kid recognized them and knew where he was.

"Gettin' up all right," he muttered, sniffing at the air. It was cold, but it had the unmistakable tang of spring. He spoke to the horses and got them moving.

The trail became steeper and he had to stop at shorter intervals.

In several places the trail was completely washed out, the runoff flowing across it and cutting a channel. The horses slithered through it, old Bess putting out a foreleg and trying to test every step before she took it.

They topped the last rise finally and were on the rim, with the Flat and camp just ahead of them. Bess wrinkled her nose and voiced a snort of accomplishment as they passed the corral. The Kid could see the cabin. Not a light was showing.

"Must be almost midnight," he thought.

He rode up to the door and got the sack of flour over his shoulder. Staggering under its heavy load, he carried it inside. He could hear Dutch and Elmer snoring heavily. Leaving the door open, he went out to begin bringing in the other things. Out of the blackness of the room Trapnell snarled at him:

"You goin' to be all night clatterin' around

there? Git the flour and bacon in and let the rest of the stuff go till mornin'! Rain won't hurt the tinned goods!"

"I got the flour in, Joe," the Kid told him.

"Wal, put up your horses, then, and roll in!" was the surly command.

The Kid was willing enough to remove the pack from the mare and put the two animals into the corral and call it a night.

In the morning he was in the kitchen with Elmer as early as usual.

"How'd things go while I was gone, Elmer? Did you have any run-ins with Trapnell?"

Elmer shook his head. "He's hardly said a word to anyone. Bein' shorthanded, he's makin' Dutch go out this mornin'. You git the stuff on the table; we kin talk later."

The men had been gone some time before the Kid had an opportunity to bring in the potatoes and canned goods that had remained outside the door during the night. The rain had not ended until just before dawn. A grunt of dismay escaped him at what he found. The rain had not injured the cans, but it had soaked off every label. The Kid gathered up an armful and rushed inside.

"Look at that, Elmer. Look at that!" he exclaimed excitedly as he dropped the naked cans on the table. "You won't know what you're openin'!"

For the first time in his life the Kid heard Elmer

laugh. The big man's flabby, shapeless torso heaved and quivered with mirth. The Kid stared at him, aghast, and there wasn't a flicker of amusement in him. With half an eye he could see that this might prove to be anything but funny.

Elmer caught the look on his face and read it correctly. The laughter went out of him with marked abruptness. He said: "He told you to leave the stuff out there, didn't he? Wal, let him like it."

The Kid shook his head. "Gee, Elmer, I dunno; Joe will blame me. Try to sort this stuff out, won't you?"

Elmer tried, but without much success. Three nights later Trapnell threw down his knife and fork with a bellow of anger.

"You, Elmer!" he yelled. "What the hell is wrong here? This is the third night in a row we sit down to hominy grits and salmon! The Kid brought up tomatoes and fruit, didn't he? Why ain't we gittin' 'em? I'm sick of this damned tripe!"

"Joe, I don't like it no better than you," Elmer answered from the kitchen doorway. "But when I open canned stuff, I got to use it."

Trapnell got to his feet and kicked his chair out of the way.

"What's that got to do with it?" he demanded, rage boiling over in him. "Don't stand there givin' me an argument!"

Elmer shrugged and turned back to the kitchen. "You kin blame yoreself for what yo're gittin'," he said over his shoulder. "It was yore idea to have the Kid leave the stuff outside the other night so the rain could wash the labels off everythin' an' leave me no chancst to know what I got in my hands till I git it open."

It reached Trapnell. For a long moment he stood there, mouth open, shocked and speechless. Grady Roberts's quiet laughter cut across the charged stillness of the room. Trapnell rocked under its impact, his lips white with fury, the challenge in that mocking laughter too plain to be misunderstood.

He was around the table suddenly, his shoulders hunched and his eyes murderous. But it was toward the kitchen he charged, not toward Grady.

Horror held the Kid motionless for a moment. He leaped in front of Trapnell then and caught him by the arm.

"Gee, Joe, don't take it out on Elmer!" he pleaded. "It's like he says, he don't know what he's usin'! I shoulda covered the stuff up, Joe! It's all my fault!"

Trapnell flung him aside and started to stride on. Just as suddenly he whirled and came back to the Kid.

"Why, you ornery little scut, what do you mean, tryin' to tell me where to head in?" he blazed. "I'll put the two of you in yore place!"

His right hand flashed out. It caught the Kid on the chin and stretched him flat on the floor. The sickening thud of Trapnell's fist crashing into the boy's face spun Elmer around like a top. Glassy-eyed, his loose cheeks the color of dead ashes, he saw the Kid go down. The big man had always feared Joe Trapnell. He feared him now; but as he saw him standing over the Kid, waiting for him to get up so that he could slap him down again, Elmer was no longer afraid. In fact, he was no longer himself. Save for one thought, his mind was blank: the Kid had tried to protect him; it was now his turn to protect the Kid.

A butcher knife lay on the kitchen table. Repeated sharpenings had worn the blade down to less than half its original width. Elmer snatched it up in a hamlike fist and rushed at Trapnell.

The Kid still lay on the floor, half dazed. Legs were stepping over him. He knew them for Elmer's legs. He looked up. Viewed from that angle, the big man was a monstrous, misshapen hulk.

The Kid located Trapnell. Joe was backing away, stark horror stamped on his rocky face. The Kid didn't know what to make of it.

"Put down that knife, you rat!" Trapnell screamed. "Grab him, somebody!"

The Kid understood then. He scrambled to his knees, his throat dry with terror. He tried to speak, but the words wouldn't come. There was a movement of Elmer's right arm.

Trapnell tried to say something. It was unintelligible. The stiffness went out of his knees. Elmer seemed to be holding him up. It was only for a moment. He backed away, and Trapnell tumbled to the floor.

In the pin-drop silence Grady Roberts bent down over Trapnell. Old Dutch got down on the other side. Their faces, hard and flat, were dark and obscure with their thinking.

Grady said, "This was to have been my job. But I wanted the truth out of him about Steve first."

"Is he dead?" Dutch asked.

Grady nodded. "He's as dead as he ever will be."

The knife fell from Elmer's hand and clattered on the floor. His voice pinched and unfamiliar, he said, "He won't hit you agin, Kid . . . He won't hit nobody no more. . . ."

4

Fear of the consequences of what he had done began to run through Elmer. This wasn't Wyoming of the eighties; this matter did not end here.

"Aw God," he sobbed, terror gripping him. "I didn't mean to kill him. I—I—uh—jest wanted to keep him from beatin' the Kid."

The Kid turned his eyes away; he couldn't bear to look at him with his face like that. He knew Elmer had done this thing to protect him. They wouldn't be going to Cain Springs now; their pleasant dreamworld lay in ruins.

"Pull yourself together, Elmer—please!" he pleaded.

Grady got up and led the big man to a chair at the other end of the room. Dutch remained his practical self, closing Trapnell's staring eyes and covering the body with an old overcoat.

"The Kid's right, Elmer," Grady said; "you've got to pull yourself together. If ever a rat needed killing, he did. You did this corner of Wyoming a favor. But the law won't look at it that way—not the kind of law we've got in this country. Chalk

Daggett was his pal. He'll never let up on you as long as he's deputy sheriff."

Elmer rolled his head from side to side, too bewildered to use his limited mental equipment. "I don't know what to do," he moaned. "I don't know what to do."

"The best thing is to light out for Montana and keep on goin' when you git acrost the line," Dutch advised. "Take enough grub to last you a few days and help yoreself to a horse. I won't start below to tell the old man what happened till after you pull out. He'll git word into the Flat. That'll give you at least a day's start."

Elmer just sat there, shoulders drooping, breathing heavily. "Where's the Kid?" he asked.

"Right here, Elmer," the boy answered, a quaver in his voice that he could not control.

The big man turned and gazed at him pathetically.

"Gee, I spoiled everythin', didn't I, Kid—all our plans."

"That's all right, Elmer; we're still pardners. You do as Dutch and Grady say."

The Kid's glance went to Roberts.

"I'm goin' with him, Grady. He did this on my account."

"No, Kid, don't make that mistake," the tall man told him. "You're in the clear; Daggett can't touch you. That won't be the case if you help Elmer make a getaway."

The Kid shook his head uncompromisingly.

"I got to go, Grady. What could he do by himself? They'd nab him before he'd got forty miles."

Roberts knew that was true. He couldn't imagine Elmer keeping ahead of the law for long. That would take "savvy," and the man didn't have it. The Kid had plenty of it.

"Yo're wastin' yore time arguin' with him, Grady," Dutch advised. "I know the Kid; he's got his mind made up. He'll go."

"I suppose he will," the tall man observed grimly. "A friend sticks, they say; that's the way the Kid seems to be built—more credit to him." He didn't know what lay behind Elmer's talk of plans gone awry or the boy's statement that the two of them were still partners, but it said there was a bond between them, and that was enough for Roberts.

"Kid, do you know anything about Chalk Daggett?"

"I know he's a dirty, schemin' blackleg. Trapnell was his pal, wasn't he? That'd be enough for me."

"Trapnell was just a first-class rat, Kid, without any brains; Daggett is really dangerous. He'll hang onto this like a bulldog. There isn't anything he'll stop at if he thinks it will help his game. I want you to remember that . . . Do you know this country north of here?"

"Purty good. I'll find a way through. We can go up the—"

"Better keep it to yourself, Kid," Grady cut him off. "Map out something and stick to it. You want to ditch the horses as soon as you can; they'll be wearing the brand and it'll be a dead giveaway if you're seen . . . Dutch, you get Elmer to wrap up some grub; I'll walk down to the corral with the Kid."

He took Trapnell's saddle and bridle; the Kid shouldered his own battered kak. Elmer would need a big horse to carry him; the Kid tossed his saddle on the pony he used on his trips below. It took only a few minutes.

Roberts pressed a ten-dollar gold piece into the boy's hand. "You'll need a little money, Kid."

The youngster steadied his voice before he spoke. "I reckon I won't be seein' you again, Grady."

His defenses failed him, and though he set his teeth against it, his voice faltered. For the moment he was just a boy and not the man he usually successfully pretended to be. What Roberts was able to read in the Kid's eyes tightened his mouth. He had been aware for a long time that in a mild way he had taken the boy's fancy, but he realized now that it went much deeper than that.

"Chances are you'll be back in Wyoming one of these days," he said encouragingly. "Let's wait and see how things work out. I'll be around, Kid;

I've got some unfinished business with Daggett that'll keep me here."

The boy nodded woodenly and got a better grip on himself. "If I ever come back I'll look you up . . . Don't let Daggett tie you into this, Grady."

"No," Roberts answered, touched by the lad's concern for him. "He won't get very far with that. But don't you worry about me; you look out for yourself, Kid. And don't let this trouble throw you; you keep to the straight and narrow till I see you again."

They led the horses to the cabin. Elmer and Dutch were waiting. There were no good-bys, no backward glances; the Kid and Big Elmer just rode away into the night. If the latter had had his way, their flight would have been headlong. The Kid said no; they had to use their wits.

He knew the Big Medicines were not safe for them, and he was equally aware that they were leaving a trail in the mud that a child could follow. Knowing there was nothing they could do to hide it, he did the next best thing, repeatedly making it appear that they were trying to find a way down the western slope so they could break through to the Tetons or the Hole. Other men had found refuge in that wild, tangled country south of the Park. Their pursuers would know it, too, and could expect them to go that way. The Kid told himself it was the best reason in the world for heading in another direction.

Shortly after midnight they crossed a long, bare saddle. A wet, sticky snow began to fall, blotting their trail. Hope soared high in the Kid; he had not expected to see snow again that spring. The creeks were all flowing to the east now. It told him how far they had come. They put their horses into one of the creeks and followed it for half a mile.

Confident that they had broken their trail, the Kid became less cautious. They moved faster. When morning came they were on the headwaters of the Greybull. The snow had turned to rain. They picketed their spent broncs and crawled under a tarp and slept for several hours. The Kid made Elmer eat a bite; he didn't risk a fire for coffee.

For the rest of that day their way led north. They saw no one. Elmer was as weary as the ponies. The Kid refused to call a halt; time was precious now. Just before evening he relented and they rested for an hour. Only a tongue-lashing persuaded Elmer to take to the saddle for the rest of the night.

The second morning found them on the Stinking Water in the Wapiti Mountains. They had put almost a hundred miles behind them. But flight ended there for the time being; the right hind leg of Elmer's bronc was swollen to twice its normal size. With a gasp of dismay the Kid flung himself from the saddle to examine it. It was a bad sprain, perhaps a pulled tendon. The big bay had evidently twisted the leg by stepping into a crevice in the rocks or missed its footing in the down timber they had come through about midnight.

"Gee whiz, Elmer," he scolded, "you must have felt him favorin' this leg for hours! Why didn't you say somethin'? We coulda stopped!"

Elmer shook his head. His eyes were as dull and lusterless as a wet slate. "I didn't feel nuthin', Kid. I just figgered he was gittin' tuckered out . . . It's bad, huh?"

"You bet it's bad!" the Kid growled. A lame horse was bound to complicate matters for them; perhaps seriously. "We gotta find a place where we can hide out till the bay is fit to travel again. Why you can't use your head a little, Elmer, I dunno!"

Elmer winced, and his drooping shoulders sagged a little lower. "Don't throw it into me like that, Kid," he pleaded. "I been tryin' to do as you tell me."

"I'm sorry, Elmer; I know you're tryin'." Sight of the big man's haggard face, with its look of utter hopelessness, stabbed him and made him ask himself how they were going to make out. "You see that big clump of aspens halfway down the slope? We'll hide out there for today."

"I thought we was goin' to ditch the hosses," said Elmer. "That's what Grady Roberts told you."

"Not yet—not for three, four days. There's ranch country ahead of us. I want to slip through by night. We've got to have horses to do it." He scanned the river and the ridge and shook his head uneasily. "I don't like havin' to hole up here. We won't stay an hour longer than we have to. If we only had a safe place to—"

An idea flashed in his mind and his eyes brightened with the light of discovery.

"Elmer—we're just east and south of the Sand Hills! We're goin' to Cain Springs! We'll be safe there till the bay is right again. Yes, sir! Wonder why I didn't think of it before. By tomorrow evenin' he'll be fit enough to get you that far."

He honestly believed they would be safe enough for a while once they reached the Springs. But in saying the bay would be able to travel in another thirty-six hours, he was only voicing a hope. With sound horses, the dash into the Sand Hills could be accomplished in five hours. Even a lame horse should be able to do it between dark and dawn.

They left the river and made a dry camp among the aspens. Elmer stretched out on the ground and slept soundly. But not the Kid. He dozed off repeatedly, sleeping a few minutes and then popping awake to scan the river bottom and the main ridge of the mountains. It was impossible for him to calculate how far Elmer and he were ahead of pursuit. It depended on how many men

Daggett had out looking for them, and whether they had picked up the trail of the fugitives and were following it around by the headwaters of the Greybull or were just fanning out over the country. The Kid knew that if the latter were the case some of the possemen could be on the Stinking Water by now.

The day passed without bringing anyone, however. Just before evening the Kid stole up the slope and made a careful reconnaissance. The sun had been shining all day and the flinty soil was hard underfoot on the barren, wind-swept ridge.

With the eyes of an eagle he started to scrutinize the ridge and was jerked to piercing attention. Far off to the west three riders were sky-lined. They were working the country carefully. He knew what they were looking for.

The Kid remained on the ridge until darkness fell and put an end to their searching for the day. Since the main ridge of the Wapitis was the quickest way out of these mountains and the one that hunted men would be most likely to use, he believed the possemen would stay on it, working the side country as they moved along.

"They'll just about camp where they are tonight and start headin' this way a little after sunup," he told himself. "We got to get out of here tonight!"

Thought of the lame horse wrung a groan out of him and sent him scurrying down the slope.

Elmer had made a small fire. The Kid stamped it out in a hurry.

"No fire tonight, Elmer!" he rapped. "We ain't alone in these hills!"

Elmer snapped out of his daze and sucked in his breath in a noisy, fear-ridden gasp. The Kid didn't wait to answer any questions; the horses were tethered a few yards away, and he went to them at once and ran his hand over the bay's ailing leg. The animal flinched at his touch, though the swelling had gone down.

"Gee, that's tough!" the Kid muttered. "Another twenty-four hours and he'd be fairly fit to go."

That didn't solve their problem. Immediate flight was imperative now, and the bay was certainly not equal to it.

The Kid whipped around to find Elmer at his elbow, his saddle on his shoulder.

"Kid—if they're close, we gotta go!"

The boy shook his head.

"Put down your saddle, Elmer. We got twenty miles to go when we pull away from here. If we went now we wouldn't get across the Pitchstone Road before this bronc played out on us. We'll have to take a chance to stick it out here till the crack of dawn."

He told Elmer what he had seen on the ridge. Terror began to run away with the big man. The Kid lost all patience with him.

"Don't you go on like that, Elmer!" he warned

fiercely. "We'll be all right here for a few hours."

Elmer wasn't convinced.

"Why'n't we leave the hosses and go ahead on foot? We can walk to the Sand Hills, Kid!"

"Leave the broncs here for them to find?" the Kid demanded with furious sarcasm. "They'd be after us in a flash! You let me handle this; I know what's best. We got a little grub left. Let's eat it."

The hours passed slowly as they waited. The Kid did not risk a cigarette; he was suspicious of every sound and smell that reached him. Sitting there, busy with his thoughts, one thing kept recurring to him—he had to make plans; just sitting there waiting for daylight wouldn't do.

He made a decision finally. Out of a long silence he said, "Elmer, we gotta split up."

The big fellow stared at him, aghast.

"When it begins to grow light you're goin' to take my pony and get across the river," the Kid continued. "You keep headin' north till you hit the road. You get across it and keep goin' for a mile, then turn west toward the Sand Hills. Y'understand?"

Panic had seized Elmer. "Kid, I don't want you to leave me! I don't want to go alone!"

"You gotta do it my way, Elmer." The Kid was all iron now. "If you wasn't sure to get lost, I'd make you go right now. With daylight, you can find your way; you'll know the Pitchstone Road when you see it. Keep above it till you get close to Cain Springs. And don't you go into the house when you get there, understand? You lay out in the hills about a half a mile. There's always some wind blowin' in the hills; it'll cover your tracks."

Elmer did not answer. Only his heavy, labored breathing broke the stillness.

"You don't want 'em to get you, do you?" the Kid whipped out crossly.

"Where you goin' to be, Kid? Where you goin' to be?"

The Kid had his answer ready.

"I'll be up on the ridge. I'll let these possemen see me. That'll draw 'em off and give you a better chance." Purely for Elmer's benefit he added, "I'll play tag with them all mornin'. If they get too close, I'll turn down into the timber and shake them off."

He didn't believe anything of the sort. But that was a matter that concerned only himself. Elmer, for all of his terror, wasn't fooled.

"Don't do it, Kid!" he pleaded earnestly. "Don't do it! You'll never make it on that bronc! They'll pick you up for shore!"

"Look here, Elmer," the boy stormed, "are you goin' to be stubborn about this? Are you goin' to be stubborn, or do what I tell you? I been right so far, ain't I?"

"Yeh—"

"Gee," the Kid boasted scornfully, "you don't have to worry about me! Chances are I'll be at the Springs before you are." Hoping to clinch his argument, he added, "I don't weigh nothin'. The big bay can carry me all right; it won't be like he was packin' you."

"I hadn't thought of that," Elmer admitted, relieved. "Yo're smart, Kid, you figgered everythin' out!"

Dawn was a long time coming. With the first streak of light the Kid got to his feet. He made Elmer repeat the instructions he had given him.

"That's right; you've got everythin' straight," the Kid told him. "You wait at the Springs till tomorrow mornin'. If you don't see nothin' of me by then, you pull out for the north."

Elmer gave an anxious start. "Any chancst I won't be seein' you?"

"You'll be seein' me; I'm just tellin' you what to do in case they cut me off and I can't get there right away. Here's the ten bucks Grady gave me. You keep it. If you have to head north alone, don't you go into any ranch house for grub; you take a notch in your belt and keep on movin'. It's only about forty miles to the railroad after you get across the line. You'll hit some town where you can grab a train. Don't ride in; cache the saddle and bridle and turn the bronc loose, then walk into town and buy a ticket to Billings. It's a good time of the year for you to catch on with some outfit around there. That'll be where I'll look for you."

The Kid put his saddle on the bay. Elmer wasted several minutes adjusting the cinch on the smaller horse. The Kid gave him a hand.

"All right, swing up and get goin'!" he ordered gruffly, determined to get the parting over with as quickly and painlessly as possible. "There's open country down there, and you want to be across it before the light gets strong."

Elmer would have hung back, but the boy hurried him off with a flinty "So long!" and stood watching him until the mist rising from the river enveloped him.

"I sure hope he makes it!" he muttered huskily. "He was never cut out for anythin' like this!"

He thought he heard Elmer crossing the stream. Picking up the reins, he led the bay up the slope in the thinning ground fog. It was getting lighter by the second. He looked around for cover. A rock outcropping was the best he could find. There he waited until the sun was above the horizon.

The morning broke clear, the warm rays of the sun making short work of the mist. In a few minutes the Kid could see a long way. He scanned the ridge intently. Nothing moved. Strain his eyes as he would, he failed to catch a glimpse of the possemen. Strangely enough, it did not reassure him; the feeling was strong in him that they were very close.

"Bein' careful about showin' themselves this

mornin’,” he said to himself. “Like as not they smelled Elmer’s fire last evenin’.”

He could read signs. He studied the ground carefully but found no evidence that anyone had passed during the night.

“They’re here, all right,” he concluded grimly. “They will jump me as soon as I ride out.”

Nothing was to be gained by waiting. He made his way back to his horse. The big bay favored its lame leg even as it stood there, head lowered dejectedly. The Kid’s mouth locked a little tighter.

“I better get movin’ before I lose my nerve,” he muttered grimly.

Swinging up into the saddle, he rode out boldly. But the expected did not happen; no one cried out for him to halt or throw up his hands; no leaden messenger whined a lethal warning over his head.

The Kid shook off his surprise and glanced back along the ridge. What sort of a game was this? he wondered. What were they waiting for? They must have seen him. To remove any doubt about it, he rode in the posse’s direction—fifty yards, a hundred. It failed to produce any sign of the man hunters.

Suddenly the meaning of it dawned on the Kid: the possemen had seen something that had pulled them off the ridge. With sickening conviction he realized that something must have been Elmer. Anxiety swelled to horror in an instant and broke out on him in a cold, clammy sweat. His own safety forgotten, he swung the bay and hurried back to the spot where he had climbed the slope. Down below, the river trees thinned and he could see the wide strip of meadowland across the Stinking Water.

What he saw wrung a groan of sheer agony from him. At the far edge of the meadows, a man, too large for the pony he was riding, was fleeing toward the north. Even at that distance there was no question but that it was Elmer.

From different directions three men were after him and rapidly closing in, with one outdistancing the others. Elmer wasn't any sort of a rider; his pony was fagged. The Kid knew it could only be a matter of minutes before he was overtaken.

The posseman closest to Elmer must have known it, too, but that wasn't good enough for him. He was riding with his rifle across his saddlebow. The piebald bronc he was astride made identification easy; the Kid knew it was Chalk Daggett himself.

"No!" the boy cried as Daggett whipped the rifle to his shoulder and fired. The first shot was wild; a second shot found its mark. Elmer tumbled from his saddle and lay on the ground, a still and grotesque shape. The gunfire rolled up to the Kid, flat and evil, and reached out into the far corners of the mountains.

A sob racked the boy; no one was watching, so he didn't have to hide his misery and outrage.

"Elmer—aw-w-w, Elmer!" he whimpered, voicing all the misery that was in him. "I didn't mean for it to happen this way!"

He knew he had sent him riding right into their hands and to his death.

Daggett and the other two got down from their horses and stood gazing at the blob of stiffening flesh. The Kid watched them with blurred eyes. His thoughts ran back to Grady Roberts, who was so sure that Daggett and Trapnell had murdered his friend, Steve Ennis. This was murder too—shooting down an unarmed man who had no chance of making his escape. That fact cut through the welter of emotion and despair that gripped the boy, and he realized that Grady and he had a common goal now, one purpose to guide them.

It steadied the Kid and gave him courage. Gone was the feeling of not caring what happened to him, of giving himself up; he had to get away so that he might come back someday and help Grady to square their mutual account against Daggett.

To go, and go quickly, became uppermost in his mind. The bay would carry him a few miles. He'd give up any idea of trying to reach Montana; instead, he'd turn back toward the Greybull and head for Wind River Basin. Chalk Daggett and his men would have to do some looking to find him!

He'd need food—he had eaten only a bite or two since leaving Camp Number 3—but he wouldn't risk stopping at even a lonely mountain cabin for a day or two.

He said a wordless good-by to Elmer, and with a last glance in the direction of the Sand Hills, he left the ridge and picked his way down into the scrub timber.

5

The Kid found his way back to the Greybull. Two days and a night later he was in the Owl Creek Mountains. Though he saw no more of the posse, he continued to move warily. If his progress was slow, it was only because of the condition of his horse; he knew he would have desperate need of the bay if he was ever to reach Wind River Basin. Coaxing a few miles at a time out of the animal was as much as he dared risk.

In desperate need of food by now, he started looking for a cabin. Late in the afternoon he found one.

A faint trace of wood smoke was rising from the chimney, proof that someone was at home. Hungry as he was, he studied the place for half an hour before he rode in.

An old man stepped out as he got down. He had his rifle cradled in his arm. His manner was unfriendly, even suspicious.

"Who are yuh, boy?" he demanded, running an eye over the bay and finding and recognizing the brand on the right stifle.

"I'm just a ranch kid on my way down to the

Basin. I'm powerful hungry. I ain't no grub-line rider; I'll cut some wood for you and work out a meal."

The old man shook his head.

"I ain't needin' no wood cut. Thet's a Flat Iron bronc yo're ridin'. Yuh workin' for Flat Iron?"

"I am," the Kid replied, deciding the lie was necessary. "You acquainted with Reb Corson?"

The old man left the question unanswered, but giving him the foreman's name had helpful effect.

"Yo're right young fer a big outfit to be sendin' that fur," he observed. "What yuh goin' to the Basin about?"

The Kid had an answer ready.

"I'm lookin' for a roundup cook Reb wants."

An old woman appeared in the doorway. "Paw," she said, tucking up her scraggly hair, "yuh don't have to question the boy; he looks all right to me. We kin give him a meal . . . I'll fry yuh a piece of meat, sonny."

There was only the log cabin here; no cultivated land, no sign of livestock, not even a horse. It didn't prove anything to the Kid; like as not, the old man had three or four broncs penned up in a hidden corral out in the timber. How the couple scratched a living was no great riddle, either. In these mountains a man didn't have to worry about taking meat; a deer or bear could be knocked down almost any time. During the winter months, when fur was prime, a trap line would produce some income. But there were other ways, and easier ones, to make both ends meet; the main owl-hoot trail between Brown's Park, in Colorado, and Montana ran through this wild country on the upper reaches of Owl Creek. Rustlers and outlaws paid well for favors received.

There wasn't any doubt in the Kid's mind but that the cabin was a way station for the lawless, where they could be sure to find a meal and a fresh horse, if needed. He felt it accounted for the old man's attitude.

The Kid let him put all the questions; for himself, he knew his role was to say and see as little as possible. He felt he could safely discuss the condition of his mount. He had an explanation for the bay's lame leg, wholly fictitious.

"Slowin' me up considerable," he declared.

The old man nodded. "Yuh shouldn't be ridin' him . . . When did yuh leave the ranch?"

"Day before yesterday. I expected to be through the mountains by now."

"Hev yuh seen anyone?"

"Nary a soul."

The questioning continued, but the Kid was too smart to be tripped. He was relieved, however, when the old woman called him in and sat him down to a generous venison steak and cold spoon bread.

"Yuh was right hungry, sonny," she observed, watching him eat. "Thar's more meat in the pan, iffen yuh can eat it." The Kid had taken her eye. "We don't see many young'uns," she continued. "How old be yuh?"

"Goin' sixteen, ma'am."

"An' out makin' yore own way! Reckon yuh is an orphant."

The Kid told her he was. "There's worse things than bein' an orphan, ma'am. I been doin' all right for myself and sorta lookin' ahead."

"Sounds to me like yuh got gumption enough to git ahead, sonny." The old woman wagged her head approvingly and turned to her husband. "Don't he sound like our Willie, Paw? He was goin' to git ahead too." Her faded eyes flashed with a sudden anger. "Iffen yuh'd only given him a chancst! Yuh never was of a mind to see him grow up to be anythin' but worthless and no-account like yoreself!"

"Woman, keep yore tongue still and let the young'un eat and be on his way!" was the violent, threatening retort.

The Kid knew this was an old quarrel that didn't concern him, but he smiled in his plate as he saw the old man beat a retreat. It told him who was really boss here.

The old woman continued to hover over him, and when he was ready to leave she gave him meat and bread enough to last him several days.

He found her husband waiting for him outside, ready with another question.

"Yuh comin' back this way, boy?"

"Depends on where I find the man I'm lookin' for."

"Supposin' yuh try Crazy Woman Pass on yore trip back," was the cryptic suggestion. "She'll be open in a day or two. An' yuh keep it to yoreself that we took yuh in and fed yuh."

The Kid nodded and waved them good-by.

"Rustler hangout, sure as shootin'," he said to himself as he rode away. "If Daggett is trailin' me, he won't get nothin' out of them."

He camped that night on a creek whose name he didn't know. He felt safe enough to build a small fire and broil a piece of meat. The flow of the creek was to the southeast. It told him he was over the crest of the mountains.

He saw several cabins the following day and circled around them. The trail become more distinct. With morning he caught a distant glimpse of a small mountain ranch and knew he was moving into Wind River Basin.

Immediately the Kid found new problems confronting him. He took it for granted that Chalk Daggett, without bothering to consult old Hoke Tuller, had long since flashed word around Wyoming by telegraph, asking all sheriffs and marshals to pick him up. If so, there had been time for that word to reach every crossroads settlement in the Basin. Then, too, there was the matter of the bay. Grady had said to turn the horse adrift. Even so, the Kid was loath to do it. Flat Iron owed him the equivalent and its value; his winter's wages, which could never be collected.

He considered altering the brand but could find no way to do it; even experienced "rewrite men" had never done it successfully. Some sort of decision had to be reached, and in the end the boy resolved on a compromise: he would move carefully for the rest of the day, ride all night, and part company with the bay at daylight.

"I'll be purty far down the Basin by then," he mused. "That'll give me a better chance of gettin' a job somewheres."

He realized how much his safety depended on locating work quickly. In a country where everyone rode, a boy on foot, toting a worn saddle, would draw attention. Then, too, if he "belonged" somewhere, fewer questions would be asked about him.

He was without food again. During the day several ranch houses looked inviting, but he kept his distance. That evening a faint glow in the sky told him he was near a town.

"Must be Powder City," he concluded. He had heard punchers mention the place, about the size of Medicine Flat. According to their tales, Powder City was the liveliest town in the Basin, with a dozen outfits doing their hiring there.

The Kid was correct in thinking this was Powder City. He was several miles beyond the town when he turned back, his course clear in his mind. He would set the bay adrift and bed down somewhere on the outskirts. In the morning he would go in and try to find a job.

Hunger, as much as anything else, was driving him now. When he found a tiny creek that promised to lead him where he wanted to be for the night, he pulled his gear off the horse and gave it a slap on the rump that sent it loping away. Shouldering his saddle, he moved along the creek for half a mile. There were willow brakes along the little stream. Ahead, through the trees, he caught the gleam of a campfire. He paused and listened carefully, expecting to catch the rise and fall of voices, which, if it did nothing else, would tell him how many men were camped there.

Not a voice reached him, but he caught the scraping of a pan and the appetizing aroma of frying meat. He sniffed at it deeply, trembling as the familiar tang of burned beef struck his nostrils. Under its lash he took half a dozen steps forward before caution caught up with him.

"Better see what I'm walkin' into!" he warned himself.

Without attracting attention he proceeded a few yards and was finally able to see the camp. An old man of tremendous size, his white hair cascading over his broad shoulders and a long white beard half concealing his ruddy face and giving him the benevolent look of a character out of the Bible, was bending over the fire, cooking his supper. A spring wagon, covered with a canvas tilt in the fashion of a prairie schooner, stood a few feet beyond the fire. The spavined mules that drew it were grazing contentedly on the lush grass along the creek bank.

The Kid studied the old man for a moment.

"Bet he's either a gospel shark or a medicine peddler," he said to himself. "He's old, but he don't look like he'd ever worked himself to death."

It was a shrewd and accurate surmise, for Isaiah Smith was both a hell-fire-and-brimstone street-corner revivalist and herb doctor, depending on which calling he found most profitable at the moment. For forty years he had been a bird of passage, moving across Wyoming, Idaho, Nevada, and half a dozen other Western states in search of an easy dollar. Hundreds of little Powder Cities had known him. If the list was long it was due to his necessity of seeking new and greener pastures every season, since he had long ago found it expedient never to return to a town once visited.

Which of his dual roles he was to assume in any given place depended on what he learned on his arrival. If he found that some brother evangelist had just left town, he made his pitch as the discoverer of the one and only Golden Elixir, guaranteed to cure all the ills man was heir to; if a medicine show had been there recently, skimming off the cream in that field, the Golden Elixir remained in the trunk and he sold religion.

When possible, he camped on the outskirts of a town, as he was doing now. He had walked into Powder City that afternoon and made certain inquiries. The information he gained had convinced him that what Powder City needed was gospel.

Rogue that he was, Isaiah liked himself best as a worker in the vineyard of the Lord. His sonorous voice was well suited for the part. When he raised it against sin and the remissness of men, it took on a commanding rumble. At the proper moment—and it usually came about the time he was ready to hand out a little printed tract and pass the hat—the great voice melted to honeyed unctuousness that seldom failed to bring in a few shekels. He knew the Bible backward, as the saying goes, and whenever he was to essay the role of revivalist, even his casual speech became as thickly studded with amens and hallelujahs as a rice pudding with raisins.

Standing on the lowered back platform of his wagon attired in a knee-length Prince Albert, now faded to a dull bottle green, the scene illuminated by a pair of gasoline flare lamps, face uplifted and his snow-white beard and hair tossed by the wind, he presented such a picture of hoary benevolence that men paid him a reverent respect even though many of them slunk away without contributing a two-bit piece to further the great "work" in which he was engaged.

Having made a few purchases in Powder City, he had returned to the wagon and got out two cloth signs and attached them to the sides of the tilt.

The firelight struck one of the signs, and the Kid read the legend with interest.

Blessed Are Those Who Seek the Lord!
THE NEW RESURRECTION
GOSPEL WAGON
Rev. Isaiah Smith, Prop.

"A sky pilot, just as I figured," the Kid commented to himself. "Bet the old slipper-tongue will have me workin' half the night for a plate of meat and beans!"

He kicked a dry limb deliberately so that Isaiah would be aware of his approach.

"Evenin' to you, Parson," he said, walking up to the fire. "Smelled your cookin' half a mile up the crick. I'd sure appreciate bein' invited to sit down with you and have a bite."

Isaiah was averse to offering any hospitality to panhandlers and stray humans whenever they wandered into a camp of his, and he was about to refuse the boy's bid, but on looking him over carefully and noting his wistful face and the wisdom in the Kid's hungry-looking eyes, an idea flashed in his mind that made him reverse himself.

"As a humble wayfarer of the Lord, I will be delighted to share my meager repast with you, young man. Put down your burden and rest yourself; supper will be ready in just a minute."

The Kid draped his saddle and bridle over a wagon wheel and went to the creek and washed his face and hands, drying himself with his shirt. He didn't care particularly for the old man's lingo; otherwise, the Reverend Smith struck him as a halfway decent old juniper.

"Suppose you rest and let me finish the cookin'," he volunteered. "I'm right handy around a fire."

Isaiah's interest in him grew, and he was easily persuaded to sit back and let the Kid take over his chore.

"I reckon I was right, callin' you Parson," the latter remarked. "You are the Reverend Smith?"

"None other, son! None other! What is your name?"

"David," the Kid answered after a moment's hesitation.

"David!" Isaiah pronounced it dramatically. "It's a powerful name, son! A powerful name! Are you a town boy?"

"Nope, I'm an all-around range hand. Do most anythin' that ain't too heavy for me. I figured I'd bed down along here tonight; I want to go into town in the mornin' and try to rustle a job."

Isaiah nodded and said nothing, but his mind was busy. The Kid brought him a heaping plate of beefsteak and beans.

"Wind River Basin is your home range, I presume, son?"

"More or less you might say it is," the boy answered cagily. "I go most anywheres . . . I'll bring the coffee over."

They talked as they ate. The more the Kid had to say, the more clearly Isaiah realized that the boy could be very valuable to him. He usually hired some local youngster to pass out the tracts and take up the collection. In those towns where he sold the Golden Elixir he had always felt the need of a little entertainment on the wagon. He carried a small organ and, lacking a trusted assistant, had to play it himself. This boy, with his old man's air and pinched face, had something about him that would appeal to an audience. Isaiah was showman enough to sense it. He could teach him how to play the organ, sing hymns in one town and minstrel tunes in the next.

Truly, it seemed to the old faker that he had come upon a pearl of great price. After supper, when the Kid got out his mouth organ and made sad, plaintive sounds on it, fashioning a melody of his own, Isaiah was sure of it. A boy to cook his meals, drive the wagon, look after the mules, and a valuable assistant on the platform as well, he could ask for nothing more.

With great adroitness he tried to draw the boy out about himself. He met with no success. The Kid's evasiveness prompted the surmise that he was in trouble and undoubtedly running away from it. Isaiah was interested only because he believed he could turn it to his advantage.

"David, if it's a job you want, you need look no further. You can come on the wagon with me. It is an exciting life on the wagon, always moving on to another town, seeing new faces, camping wherever night overtakes us."

The Kid couldn't believe his good luck; here was a job that would get him out of Wyoming and far beyond Chalk Daggett's reach until such time as it was safe to return. For all his excitement, he managed to repress his eagerness to say yes and asked what his work would be.

Isaiah made light of the chores and dwelt at length on the little organ and how he would teach the Kid to play it.

"It is not always possible for me to do the Lord's work," he confessed. "In some towns I offer my wonderful Golden Elixir for sale. Such times call for a little lively entertainment, David—a minstrel song, your mouth organ. I have a gold-braided coat that can be made to fit you. It's a fine life for a boy! A fine life! I haven't said anything about wages. I will pay you a dollar a week and found. At the end of the season you will have a comfortable sum coming to you."

It was a sum, needless to say, which he could contrive never to deliver. The Kid missed that point, but he sensed the duplicity in appearing in one town as a minister of the gospel and in the next as a medicine man.

"Where would we be headin' when we leave Powder City?" he asked.

"Down toward Lander and out across Idaho."

Isaiah noted the lad's relief and was further convinced that the youngster was getting away from something unpleasant.

"Well, what do you say, David?"

"Reckon I'm your man. How long do you figure it'll be before we hit Idaho?"

Isaiah smiled to himself, sure of the reason that prompted the question. "In about ten days to two weeks. The weather will be getting fine. We'll move right along."

The Kid began to gather up the dirty dishes.

"What am I to call you?" he asked. "Reverend Smith?"

"Suppose you just call me Gran'pap, David," was the considered answer. "That will cover everything. If anyone asks you who you are, tell him you're my grandson, David Smith."

Such an arrangement had its advantages, the Kid realized. But his eyes were open now.

"All right, Gran'pap," he declared coolly. "But you ain't foolin' me, you old faker. You ain't no more a genuine sky pilot than I be."

Old Isaiah was amused by such frankness and he leaned back and chuckled heartily.

"I'm glad we understand each other, David. That's the way for partners to start; you keep my secret and I'll keep yours."

It pulled the Kid up sharply.

"What do you mean by that, you old skinflint?"

Isaiah gave him a knowing smile.

"The law is looking for a boy whose description fits you to a T. Last week in Thermopolis I saw the notice on the board in the post office."

This was sheer invention; he had never been in Thermopolis and had not seen any notice. But he had only to watch the Kid's face to realize he had hit the nail on the head.

"Don't you want to tell me your side of it, David?"

The Kid shook his head.

"I didn't do nothin' wrong. But if they're after me, I better pull my freight."

"No, no, David; you'll be safe with me," Isaiah declared reassuringly. "I'll buy you a new outfit tomorrow. You will look different in a nice suit of clothes and a new hat. In just a few days we'll be shaking the dust of Wyoming off our boots . . .

Of course I'm taking your word for it that you didn't do anything wrong."

It was a clever bid for the Kid's confidence.

"I didn't—not accordin' to my lights," the latter responded. "I claim a pardner has to stick, no matter what comes up."

Isaiah nodded thoughtfully. A little more shrewd prodding rewarded him with the complete story of the killing of Trapnell and the flight with Elmer. It convinced him that the law was not interested in finding the Kid. However, he pretended to see serious consequences in it. He knew he had a string on the boy that now would hold him in slavery until his usefulness ended.

"You are innocent of any wrong-doing, David—it was a noble thing you did, trying to help your friend—but that won't stop the law from taking you back if it catches up with you. But don't you have any fear on that account; I'll be around to see you through. You just let me do all the necessary talking. You're my grandson; don't forget that."

The Kid found a measure of confidence in the old man's promised protection.

"He's a smooth article and knows all the tricks," he mused as he settled down to washing the dishes. "Bet he's had some brushes with the law. Reckon he can see me through, as he says."

The pots and pans got a better scouring than

they were in the habit of receiving. Isaiah watched approvingly.

"Where we supposed to be from?" the Kid turned to inquire.

"Make it Tennessee—way back in the Blue Ridge," Isaiah answered after some reflection. "That's far enough away to stop any questions."

"You won't forget about stakin' me to a new outfit, Gran'pap?"

"First thing in the morning, David. Yes, sir! We're going to do all right together, you and me! You can say 'Amen!' to that, son!"

6

The Kid was given a blanket. He curled up beneath the wagon that night. In the morning, after breakfast, Isaiah invited him to inspect the interior of the wagon, with its trunks, folding cot, and organ. There was a rack for clothing, a chest of drawers in which the ingredients that went into the Golden Elixir were kept. Everything was arranged with the greatest economy of space.

"No room to spare," the Kid commented, marveling at the arrangement.

"On a stormy night you can bunk on the floor," said Isaiah. "Let me show you the organ. Remember, you have to keep pumping it while you're playing. You have an ear for music, David; in no time at all you'll be right at home at the keyboard."

The organ was pulled out on the lowered rear platform. The Kid sat down at it and tried to produce a chord. The instrument fascinated him.

"I'm going into town now," Isaiah informed him. "After you've finished your chores you can sit down here and see what you can do."

Jeptha and Japtha, the mules, had to be curried

and brushed. They were old and decrepit. The Kid shook his head as he worked on them.

"Don't look like they'll ever get us to Idaho if some grain ain't put into 'em," he mused aloud. "You could play a tune on their ribs!"

When he had finished he peeled off his patched overalls and faded shirt and bathed in the creek. He had never owned a suit of clothes. The prospect filled him with mingled dismay and eagerness.

"Reckon I'll get used to 'em," he thought. "I wish Grady could see me when I get togged out. Bet he wouldn't know me."

Grady Roberts was seldom out of his thoughts for long. Someday, he was resolved, they would be together again and square their joint account against Chalk Daggett. If he thought less often of Elmer it wasn't because he was forgetting him and the promise he had made that morning on the Stinking Water. But for all his loyalty, he had begun to realize that the big man would never have made him the kind of partner he needed; Elmer was too slow on the draw. Perhaps it was just as well that they had never set themselves up at Cain Springs.

The Kid made the admission reluctantly.

"Won't do no good to moan over it now," was his realistic thought. "The first thing for me to do is to get myself in the clear."

Isaiah had told him they would drive into town

in the late afternoon and parade up and down the main street to let people know there was going to be a gospel meeting that evening. At the conclusion of the "services" they would pull out of Powder City and head down the Basin to the next town.

The Kid's thoughts did not go beyond Powder City. If no one recognized him there, chances were he would be safe in Washakie and Lander. Powder City would be that test. He wondered what he'd do if the marshal made his way through the crowd gathered around the wagon and snapped a handcuff on him, the way he had seen Hoke Tuller do once in Medicine Flat with a man who had taken some money from the bank.

"I won't try to run," he decided. "I'll keep my mouth shut and let Gran'pap do the talkin'. If he can't get me off, I'll go back and face it like a man."

He sat down to smoke a cigarette before going to the organ. Isaiah had told him it was all right to smoke when they were alone but never in town. Some fools held smoking to be sinful, he had said.

When the old man returned at noon, several packages under his arm, he was piped into camp to the martial strains of "Marching through Georgia." The organ stops bothered the Kid, but he had no trouble in picking out a melody. Isaiah beamed at him approvingly.

"You're doing fine, David! Excellent! Have you tried your hand at a hymn?"

"I can do 'Onward, Christian Soldiers' purty good. Course, that ain't really a hymn. I kinda had to make up parts of this one."

He played the song his mother had sung to him, eying the packages the while.

"Do you know it, Gran'pap?"

"That's an old one, David. And good! 'When All Thy Mercies' is the name of it. See if I can remember a few lines. Play it again.

"When all Thy mercies, O my God!
my rising soul surveys,
Transported with the view, I'm lost
in wonder, love and praise."

"That's it!" the Kid declared soberly. "There's lots more to it."

"Yes, she's a long one. We'll have to brush up on it. You climb into these duds now and see how you like them."

He had bought everything from boots to hat. He considered it a solid investment and had not stinted. The suit was a sedate salt-and-pepper gray; the hat a flat-brimmed black Stetson.

The new boots were a trifle narrow and pinched the Kid's feet; the suit was more than ample. But he felt strange and confined in it.

"Turn around and let me have a look at you,"

Isaiah commanded. "Well! You're a little gentleman! You don't look like the same boy, David! I wish we had a looking glass large enough so you could see yourself. How does everything feel?"

"The boots need a little breakin' in. Reckon they'll soften up after I rub some grease into 'em." He took off his coat and surveyed it with pride. "I'll just use this rig when we're havin' a meetin'; I couldn't do any work in it; I wouldn't feel right. I'll sure take good care of it," he added, his way of expressing his gratitude.

"That's right, David; keep it neat and make it last. Unless someone's snooping around camp, you needn't dress up till just before we drive into a town. We're going to have a good turnout tonight. I distributed a few handbills this morning."

The handbills served as well in one place as another, requiring only to have the location of the meeting written in a blank space at the bottom.

The Kid got back into his overalls and cooked dinner. Isaiah busied himself in the wagon. The Golden Elixir was well spiked with alcohol, and whenever he felt the need of a stimulant he downed a modest snifter of it. Today was no exception. After he had indulged himself he sat down with a worn Bible and sought some embellishments for his set harangue for the evening's meeting.

He was finished before the Kid had dinner ready. Unlocking a trunk, he brought out the gold-braided coat he had mentioned. It was part of a drum major's uniform, a bright cherry red. He stepped on the platform with it and held it up for the Kid's admiring inspection.

"It's a beauty, David! A beauty!"

He could see that it was three or four sizes too large for the boy, but he let him try it on. The Kid looked like a scarecrow in it; his hands were not visible and the epaulets sagged down over his narrow shoulders.

"It's a job for a tailor," Isaiah told him. "We'll have it attended to in Lander."

After dinner Gran'pap dozed for an hour. The Kid found a bottle of vinegar and a can of grease and went to work on the harness. Like everything else in the outfit, it was old and uncared for, the leather cracking and the brass buckles dull with tarnish.

The Kid accomplished a minor miracle on it. When Isaiah opened his eyes and beheld the results of the boy's industry, the cockles of his heart warmed with satisfaction. Truly, he had become possessed of a great treasure.

When it got to be five o'clock he told the Kid it was time to be getting started. The boy harnessed Jeptha and Japtha and put them to the wagon. He got into his new finery then. Isaiah handed him the reins.

"You do the driving, David. You'll have to favor Japtha a little; he's poorly this spring."

"They need grain, both of 'em," the Kid said flatly.

"They'll get some oats soon as the money starts coming in."

The mules made their own gait, a comfortable walk, and gave the Kid to understand that no amount of urging would induce them to break into a trot.

Soon after leaving the creek they turned into a dirt road. The wheels squealed as the wagon jolted over its uneven surface. The Kid made a mental note to grease them at the first opportunity. He could see Powder City sprawled out ahead of him.

"Don't act scared," Gran'pap said. "No one's going to recognize you."

The Kid was nervous, but after they had driven up and down the length of Powder City's main street several times and no one had rushed out to pluck him off the wagon, he began to feel easier. They turned into a side street at the corner where the bank stood and backed the wagon against the wooden sidewalk.

"It's the best corner in town," Isaiah observed. He had an eye for such things. "We can let down the platform and get things ready. I'll hang up the lamps myself; I want 'em just right. You push out the organ. I'm going to let you play that hymn to open and close the services."

As usual, some of the town's small fry had been

attracted already. Gran'pap advised them it was time to be getting home to supper, but they hung on, watching the proceedings with great curiosity until the mother of one appeared on the scene and led her protesting offspring away by the ear.

With approaching darkness, Isaiah stepped down on the sidewalk and shook hands with those passers-by who paused to give him a respectful nod.

A squat little man, a silver star pinned on his vest, stepped up to him. Isaiah towered above him like a shaggy St. Bernard looking down on a plump poodle. The Kid's face paled. He turned his back on them and overheard the marshal say, "Give 'em a good goin'-over, Parson! The skin of some of the sinners in this town is tougher'n bull hide!"

After conversing for a minute the marshal sauntered on. Isaiah caught the Kid's attention and gave him a sly, knowing wink.

The crowd began to gather. Isaiah climbed on the platform and lighted the flare lamps. The Kid took his place at the organ and began to play. The sea of upturned faces made him nervous; his new boots hurt him. Somehow, he got through the hymn without playing too badly.

A hushed silence fell as the prophet of the New Resurrection strode to the very edge of the platform and stood with arms upraised to heaven. It got him the attention he wanted.

"The Word is God, and God is the Word!"

His voice rolled out over the crowd like the booming of a cannon. Without further preamble he launched his harangue. For forty minutes he gave the devil such a lambasting as that individual had never previously received in Powder City. He likened him to a master rustler working night and day to put his loop on the unwary. The poor sinner was just a maverick, surrounded by quicksands and pitfalls of evil. Once the devil got him down and slapped his brand on him, repentance was the only thing that could save him. God was the great Sheriff of the universe; acknowledge Him and the most abandoned sinner could escape from the tomb of despair and climb the golden stairs to salvation in a glorious resurrection that would make all heaven rejoice.

The Kid had heard what he called "gospel sharks" more than once in Medicine Flat and Cody. He had never listened to one who claimed to be on such intimate terms with God and the devil as old Isaiah.

"They're eatin' it up out there," was his silent observation as he glanced at the crowd.

At a prearranged signal he got down from the platform to pass out the tracts and take up the collection. Isaiah was right: the boy's thin, wistful face did the trick; hard-shelled punchers dipped deep into their pockets and dropped a two- or four-bit piece in the hat.

The prophet was down on his knees, praying. He caught the clink of silver and his fervor increased. He knelt there until the Kid placed the collection before him. The former went to the organ and played the closing hymn. Isaiah arose then and thanked the assemblage for its bounty.

The crowd filtered away slowly. The Kid moved the organ into the wagon; Isaiah extinguished the lamps. An elderly woman, so tiny that only her head appeared above the platform, got his attention. She had a half dollar in her wrinkled hand.

Her boy was behind the walls in Laramie City for horse stealing, she said. She wanted the prophet to pray for him.

"You dirty old crook!" the Kid muttered as he saw the old man take the money.

Isaiah asked her son's name. "I'll offer a good prayer for him before I close my eyes tonight," he declared with great feeling. "Have faith, Mother; the Lord will not fail you."

The little woman thanked him and turned away, reassured.

In a few minutes the wagon was rumbling out of town. The Kid pulled off his boots before the lights were behind him.

"What a wonderful town!" Isaiah purred. "It was a grand meeting, David! A grand meeting! You were a bit nervous tonight, but you'll overcome that. We'll drive an hour or two and pull up when we reach a stream and have supper before we seek our blankets."

The Kid nodded woodenly. There was a hard, set look on his face. Gran'pap studied him craftily for a minute or two.

"Something wrong, David?" he questioned.

"You made a good haul tonight; you shouldn't have taken that old woman's four bits. She couldn't afford to give it, and you knew it!"

Isaiah nodded gravely. "Yes, I did," he acknowledged, undisturbed. "You would do well to consider that she had her reward, no matter how hard her four bits was come by. You saw her face light up. She went away happy, consoled. I would have stabbed her to the heart if I had refused her offering. Faith is wonderful, David! Wonderful!"

7

The Kid quickly got used to life on the wagon and began to like it. The work was easier than grubbing in a cook shanty or swamping out a bunkhouse. Then, too, old Isaiah was seldom cantankerous; he was close-fisted, but there was always plenty to eat, and the Kid learned how to wheedle a dime out of him now and then.

They stopped four times on their way down to Lander. The pickings were far below what they had taken in Powder City. They sold the Golden Elixir in one place, and Gran'pap became Dr. Isaiah Smith for the occasion. He had a set of cloth signs for that end of the business, similar to the ones he used when it was to be a revival meeting. Simply by attaching them to the sides of the tilt, the gospel wagon became the home of the discoverer of the great elixir. He had a set of large colored charts showing the different organs of the body. During the course of his harangue, the Kid, armed with a wooden pointer, turned the charts and Gran'pap discoursed learnedly on the functions and failures of heart, kidneys, and the like.

The Kid liked the medicine business better than the gospel meetings; he had no difficulty in drawing lively melodies from the little organ. A turn with the harmonica appealed to him too.

Lander was bigger than any place they had struck. They camped on the plains north of town, and Gran'pap went in to look things over.

"It'll have to be the elixir," he announced on his return. "A tent revival just pulled out two days ago. But we'll do all right with the medicine, David. We'll put on a good entertainment. I located a tailor who says he can cut the coat down to your size."

"When do we drive in?" the boy inquired.

"Soon as we have a bite to eat. Cook up enough so we can take along what's left over and eat it cold this evening. That'll be cheaper than going into one of the eating houses."

This was a dry camp, and the Kid had to draw the water for the coffee from a keg they carried for such an emergency.

"You settled on the spot where we're goin' to open up?" he asked. He had learned that this was important.

"There's a vacant lot across from the hotel, David. It's right in the heart of things. When we get done with the tailor I want you to pass out some handbills. We'll back the wagon up to the street and you can stand there and hand out the bills as folks go by."

Isaiah sat down in the shade of the wagon and communed with himself for some minutes. The printed price on every bottle of the Golden Elixir was one dollar. As a special "introductory offer" he usually passed it out at four bits. But Lander looked prosperous to him. "I'll make it six bits tonight and throw in a box of the corn salve," he decided. "We'll put on a good entertainment."

His attention strayed to the Kid.

"David, it's too bad you don't sing a little. One of those fast darky tunes would sure liven things up."

"Maybe I'll take up singin' one of these days," the Kid responded without interest. "It won't be none of that shoutin' stuff; I like a song to have sad words."

Isaiah shook his head. "A sad song goes fine with gospel, but it's no way to sell medicine. If you're going to be a real trouper, David, you've got to give an audience what it wants. If you got out there in that gold-braided coat, your hair slicked back and your eyes shining, and gave 'em a rip-snorting song like 'Dixie' or 'Camptown Races,' they'd just about tear the shirts off their backs for you. You've never heard such applause as there'd be."

The direct appeal to the Kid's vanity put the matter in a different light, for he had begun to like the attention he received on the platform.

"I'll have to do some practicin' before I try it," he declared. "I don't want to get out there and make a fool of myself."

"Lander's the biggest town we'll hit until we make Green River," Isaiah reminded him. "It'd be a fine place to do a little singing. You know the words to 'Dixie,' don't you?"

"Not all of 'em."

"Well, I'll write them out for you. You do a little practicing this afternoon. I'll play the organ for you. I tell you, you'll feel like singing when you slip into that red coat!"

Though Lander had a population of less than fifteen hundred, it was the biggest town the Kid had ever seen. The railroad had just built in from Casper, accounting for the wave of prosperity. Previously, trail herds from the north had driven through Lander on the way down to the shipping points on the Union Pacific. Wherever he had worked, the Kid had heard punchers tell of the high times they had had there. In a way it gave him the feeling that he was on familiar ground. The hotel and main street looked about as he had pictured them.

"Just as well the shippin' season ain't on," he said to himself. "There'd be somebody in town who'd recognize me."

When the wagon had been placed for the evening's business and the mules picketed, Isaiah led the Kid around to the tailor shop. The old

German gasped when he saw what a heroic task he had to perform.

"By golly, I have goots enough left to make the phoy a pair of pants!" he exclaimed.

Gran'pap was interested in the possibility.

"No, I'm only choking," the tailor said laughingly. "I have the coat ready for you by six o'clock."

The Kid caught a reflection of himself in a long mirror. It gave him a start. "By grab, Gran'pap's right," he thought. "Nobody'd know me in this rig! I don't even know myself!"

He tilted the black Stetson to a more rakish angle. That was the way Grady Roberts wore his hat.

After passing out the handbills for an hour he climbed into the wagon and memorized the lyrics of "Dixie."

"Let's hear you sing it once," Gran'pap ordered. "You can keep your voice down."

A canvas curtain shut off the interior of the wagon from the gaze of passers-by.

"Try it again and put a little more zip into it, David. I'll play it softly on the organ, and you keep up with me."

They ran over it a number of times until Isaiah was satisfied.

"You'll be better than all right, David!" he said. "First thing you know, I'll have to be raising your wages!"

The Kid was not proof against such flattery. "If I'm goin' to stick in this business I might as well make it amount to somethin'," he informed the old man.

Gran'pap had to go up the street to purchase fuel for the lamps before the stores closed.

"I'll pick up the coat on the way back," he promised. "You take charge till I return. You might set out a bit to eat for us."

The old man had been gone twenty minutes or more when someone rapped sharply on the platform and called: "Hello in there! I want to talk to yuh!"

The voice had authority. The Kid put down the knife with which he had been slicing a piece of cold meat, raised the curtain, and stepped out on the platform. The town marshal of Lander stood there, his face rocky behind his handlebar mustache. A chill ran down the Kid's spine; he was convinced that the marshal had come for him.

"I've had my eye on you ever since you hit town," he was informed. "Ignorance of the law ain't no excuse for breakin' it. How long you been with this outfit?"

"I don't know what you mean by that," the Kid countered craftily, though his knees were shaking. "Gran'pap brung me up."

The marshal gave him a cold glance.

"Gran'pap, eh? Where is he? I want a word with him."

"He just went down the street. He'll be back directly." The Kid had to know where he stood. "What's the law got agin me?"

The officer's business was with Isaiah, and he was about to tell the boy as much, but the latter's question made him prick up his ears.

"What's behind yore askin' me that?" he demanded suspiciously. "Are you a runaway kid that this old duffer has picked up? How shore are you that he's yore gran'pap?"

"That's what everybody calls him back home in Tennessee," the Kid answered, getting a grip on himself. "He's my gran'pap all right!"

"Tennessee, eh?" The marshal scowled. "If yuh've come that far, I reckon I ain't interested in yuh. Here's the old gent comin' now."

Isaiah recognized the law and saw at a glance that the Kid was frightened. "What's the trouble, Marshal?" he inquired ingratiatingly. "I trust the young'un hasn't done anything wrong."

"Jest stopped to tell yuh yuh can't open up tonight unless you got a license," he was told. "No peddlin' in Lander without a license. That's the new ordinance. Yuh had all afternoon to drop in to see the town clerk and pay yore two dollars."

The Kid was relieved. That was not the case with Gran'pap.

"I didn't know licenses was required," he said humbly. "I appreciate your calling it to my attention. If you will be so good as to direct me to the clerk's office—"

The marshal shook his head; he had pulled out his watch. "It's after six; Ed's locked up for the day and gone home. I'll show you his house; maybe yuh can git him to come down after supper."

The two men walked away. The Kid retreated into the wagon and plopped himself down on a trunk, so shaken that he wasn't interested in the gold-braided coat peeping from its paper wrapping. He knew he had almost given himself away.

"That was a close shave!" he muttered breathlessly. "I almost said too much. Next time a marshal comes to the wagon I won't be so quick to figure he's after me."

He collected himself and tried on the coat. Its magnificence further restored his confidence. "It sure is purty!" he thought.

Isaiah was gone a long time. The Kid was hungry. After waiting twenty minutes he decided to eat by himself. He had been finished fully half an hour before the old man returned.

"Did you get it, Gran'pap?"

"I got it." The prophet was in a black mood. He tapped his breast pocket. "These grafters are making it harder and harder for a man to earn an honest living!" he declared with self-righteous indignation. "The marshal was asking me about you. In the future, you refer the likes of him to me and keep your mouth shut, as I told you."

Though it was an unpromising beginning, the evening proved to be a banner one for the Golden Elixir. The Kid's singing and playing appealed to the crowd beyond Isaiah's expectations. After the boy had sung "Dixie" several times there were loud calls for him to render another song. There was a hurried consultation on the platform.

"I'll have to give 'em a ballad, Gran'pap; I don't know no others."

The prophet nodded reluctantly. "Take your place at the organ and give them whatever you please, but make it short."

The Kid obliged with "Come Where My Love Lies Dreaming," the "saddest" song in his limited repertoire. His clear, boyish soprano had a haunting, melancholy quality that stirred his listeners deeply. It seemed to put a spell on them, and when Isaiah made his "special introductory" offer they responded as meekly as sheep being led to the slaughter. Before they closed up shop for the night the prophet was purring louder than he ever had.

Other towns followed. A week later they were in Rock Springs. Then Green River, Granger, Bridger, and up to Kemmerer. Early in May they crossed the line into Idaho. Gran'pap no longer needed to tell the boy what to do; to the limit of the little talent he possessed, the Kid had become an accomplished performer. His mythical wages had been raised to two dollars a week, and whenever he needed two bits for tobacco or a bag of sweets, Isaiah dared not refuse him.

The old man was far too shrewd ever to mention it, but he was beginning to fear that some rival might steal the boy. In Pocatello the proprietor of a tent show had offered him a hundred dollars for David. Whenever they reached a camping ground and found another wagon there, he now invariably ordered the Kid to drive on; he didn't want him to strike up an acquaintance with other itinerants.

The Kid often argued with him about it; he craved some companionship other than Gran'pap's. Isaiah always fell back on the same reasons for keeping to themselves: the country was overrun with wagons this summer; if anything was let slip about where they were going, like as not they'd find someone had got there ahead of them. Then, too, you never could tell when one of these outfits would try to rob you.

It made sense to the Kid. He knew Isaiah kept his money in a padlocked tin box in one of the trunks. It was unquestionably a tidy sum by now, and since it included his wages, the Kid had a selfish interest in keeping it safe.

They moved westward along the Oregon Short

Line, working the railroad and Snake River towns. The Golden Elixir ran into such heavy competition that for a period of two weeks the prophet kept it in the trunk and stuck to the gospel.

They crossed and recrossed the river several times. Late one afternoon they drove up a landing and found the Snake running so high that the ferry was not operating. The cable on which it worked was several feet under water.

Three other wagons, traveling outfits like their own, were drawn up, waiting. The Kid overheard the owner of one telling another there must have been some bad storms back in Wyoming. The brown flood pouring down the Snake was a far cry from the crystal-clear mountain streams that found their way through the Big Medicines to the Buffalo Fork of the Snake. Emigrant Creek, which the Kid had forded so many times when he was at Camp Number 3, was one of them. It made him a little homesick to think that some part of the water flowing past him had come from the tiny creeks that crossed Flat Iron range.

Gran'pap spoke to the ferryman and returned to the wagon with word that it would be late morning before they could hope to get across.

"We'll pull away from here, David. I don't like the looks of these folks; that long-nosed party who opened up across the street from us in Mountain Home, in particular."

This was the usual subterfuge. Actually he was in nowise concerned about the man in question. To his surprise the Kid said, "I don't like his looks neither. Pullin' teeth, he was! Reckon he'd pull more'n your teeth if he got the chance!"

This open country was almost treeless, and they had to drop back from the ferry for upward of a mile before they found a suitable camping ground in a coulee. A fringe of aspens framed the lower rim.

"This will do nicely," Isaiah observed. "You can pick up all the wood you need for the fire."

The Kid gave Jeptha and Japtha a measure of oats. He had the mules looking better, though he complained that if he put a little fat on them one week they'd walk it off the next.

Isaiah turned in early that evening. The Kid sat up, smoking, until the fire burned low. Before he spread his blanket beneath the wagon he took a turn around camp. It was a moonlit night, with just breeze enough to set the sagebrush to nodding and keep the patchwork of black shadows changing shape. He studied them until he was convinced that no one was lurking near camp. A vague feeling of uneasiness continued to ride him, however, and after he had taken to his blanket he lay there wide-eyed for a long time, cataloguing every sound the night brought him.

He could hear the mules grazing. One of them wrinkled its nose in a nervous snort. The Kid raised his head and saw a man moving toward the wagon. It was the long-nosed quack dentist who called himself Painless Peters. He was armed.

The Kid made no sound. It was so black beneath the wagon that he knew he was in no danger of being seen. The back platform was down. Peters reached it and drew himself up. The Kid knew it would do no good to call out a warning; Isaiah didn't possess a gun.

The wagon began to tremble on its springs. The Kid could hear a struggle going on above his head. The old man groaned and evidently fell back heavily. The sharp click of a trunk being opened followed.

The Kid scrambled to his feet and sought a weapon. The endgate rod he used for a poker caught his eye. He snatched it out of the coals. It had lain there all evening, and the sharp end was red-hot.

When Painless Peters leaped down from the wagon, his gun in one hand and Isaiah's cash-box in the other, the Kid was crouched beneath the platform, ready to spring at him. With a swift lunge he jabbed the red-hot end of the iron rod into the man's rump. The smell of burning cloth and searing flesh resulted. Peters let out a yelp of agony. Gun and tin box went flying as his hands whipped around to his tortured rear. His fingers touched the poker, and he whisked them away even quicker. Bellowing with pain, he began to run. The Kid kept after him, jabbing him right and left until he was outraced. The last he saw of Painless Peters showed him speeding toward the river, a wisp of smoke following him.

"I bet he jumps in when he gets there!" the Kid rapped. "I fixed him good, by grab!"

He hurried back to camp and retrieved the padlocked cashbox and the gun. In the wagon he found Isaiah slowly regaining consciousness. Painless Peters had tapped him on the head with the barrel of his gun. Blood dripped from the wound. The Kid revived him with a dash of cold water. Seeing with his own eyes that his money was safe had an even greater restorative effect on Isaiah.

"You're a good boy, David! A fine boy! Fetch me a bottle of the elixir. I need a stimulant."

The Kid bound up the prophet's head and got him back on the cot.

"I must do something handsome for you, David," the old fraud declared earnestly, gratitude melting him to honest good will for the moment. "I don't know what I would do without you. That renegade Peters! Trying to rob me! The Lord will punish him!"

The Kid looked up from examining the gun, a cheap .44. "Better keep the gospel out of this," he said sharply. "It's up to us to look out for ourselves!"

"I wouldn't know how to use a gun," the old man protested.

"I know how to use one! I'm takin' charge of it. If anybody tries this trick again they'll hear from me. You try to go to sleep now; and no more of the elixir. You'll be tighter'n an owl if you don't stop swiggin' it!"

"Don't scold me, David!" Isaiah entreated piteously. "I'm an old man."

"That don't mean you got to be an old fool!" the Kid snapped. "You go to sleep; I'll look after things."

8

They saw no more of Painless Peters, and after ferrying across the Snake the next afternoon they headed in the direction of Caldwell and the little Idaho towns that hug the Oregon state line.

Following the foiling of the robbery, the Kid began to take more authority to himself. In his words, he was taking charge of Isaiah, and in the same fashion he had taken charge of Elmer. He didn't question but what Gran'pap was sharp as a whip about some things; in other ways he was as thick and helpless as Elmer ever had been.

Isaiah was not unaware of what was happening. He smiled in his beard and pretended not to notice, save when the Kid went too far. Then it would be: "Don't get too big for your britches, David! I'm still the head rooster around here!"

They left Idaho behind and moved into northern Nevada. Business was alternately good and bad. The weeks ran together for the Kid and he lost track of time. It gave him a start to awake one morning and find the high peaks to the north white with snow. The snow didn't last long, but it told him summer was gone; in a few weeks the roundup wagons would be going out and the busiest season of the year would be on for rangemen. He realized regretfully that he would have to miss it this time—all the excitement, the good talk around the chuck wagon in the evening, the long drive to the railroad.

"I can get along without it," he assured himself, trying to put it out of his mind. "I'm doin' all right in this business; no reason why I should want to go back."

That wasn't true, and he knew it. Above all else, there was his promise to get some measure of justice for Elmer. That would always be there to drag him back.

He thought about it all day. Things occurred to him which he had not previously considered. It made him see the situation in a new light.

"I can't go back—not now nor any time!" he acknowledged broodingly to himself as he hitched the mules for the short drive into Wells for the evening stand. "If Daggett's got a warrant out on me, he'll keep it alive. I shoulda thought of that long ago."

He wondered what had ever given him the idea that if he kept out of sight for ten months or a year things would straighten themselves out and make it safe for him to return. He had been gone almost five months. He realized a number of things could have happened in that time. Grady had what he called his "unfinished business" with

Chalk Daggett to hold him there. Perhaps that "business" had long since been settled. If so, how had the showdown been reached? And how had it resulted? Maybe Daggett was under the sod by now; perhaps Grady had had to light out for the high places himself.

His cogitation troubled and depressed the Kid. Business in Wells was poor. It was a railroad town. When the company laid off men money dried up quickly, and the Golden Elixir, even at four bits a bottle, with a box of the corn salve gratis, had no takers. The Kid blamed himself for the poor showing they made; he had no heart for the singing.

Isaiah was glum as they drove on east to find a camping place for the night. "There's something ailing you, David," he declared gravely. "You weren't yourself this evening. Did something give you a scare?"

The boy shook his head. The old man tried again.

"You ain't sick?"

"Nope."

"What is it, then?" Isaiah was beginning to lose patience.

"Been thinkin' about my home country all day. I been kiddin' myself, figurin' I might be able to go back someday. The cards will always be stacked against me."

The prophet was relieved and also annoyed

that anything so trivial had interfered with his business.

"That's right, I'm afraid," he said, keeping his annoyance to himself. "If you could go you wouldn't be happy, David. You'd long to be back with me on the wagon; this life gets into your blood."

The Kid nodded, but he was far from convinced.

"We'll be back in Wyoming before long," Isaiah continued. "We'll work a few towns we missed on the way out. When we get across the state we'll strike down through Kansas and plan to winter in Oklahoma. It's a fine place to winter; the Indians come to town regular and it's no trick to sell 'em the elixir."

The Kid wasn't interested in Oklahoma. "Why do we have to cross Wyomin'?" he demanded. "We could turn down into Utah."

Gran'pap shook his head emphatically. "That's Mormon country; I don't want any part of it! You needn't worry about crossing Wyoming; no one will bother you."

For the next two weeks they had no luck at all; salvation brought in only a dollar or two a night, and the Golden Elixir found no purchasers. The crowds that turned out were slim. The Kid played and sang his heart out to no avail.

"It ain't your fault, David," Isaiah told the boy. "It's the towns'; they've been worked too hard this summer."

He began to talk of returning to Lander, where they had done so well. The Kid was dead against it; he had his own special reasons for not wanting to be seen there during the steer shipping. But Gran'pap became more insistent.

"It's Lander!" he declared as they were closing up after another bad night. "I don't want any nonsense out of you, David!"

The Kid protested violently. He knew it was the old man's rule never to make a second appearance in a town.

"You sold a lot of that hogwash in Lander last time! They know by now that it won't even cure a bellyache! They'll be waitin' for you if you show up again!"

"I know, I know." Isaiah dismissed it with a grunt. "There's always a new crop of suckers in a place as big as Lander. At this time of the year it will be filled up with cowboys and stockmen. There's money there, and I'll risk some unpleasantness to get it. It's Lander, and that settles it!"

The Kid considered getting his saddle and bridle out of the wagon and parting company with the old man at the first opportunity. They were still forty miles to the southwest of Lander. It gave him time to think things over.

"I better stick it out," he decided. "If I pulled away now I'd only be jumpin' out of the fryin' pan into the fire."

They were two days on the way. In Lander there was great activity at the railroad corrals; clouds of dust were being kicked up by the milling steers. A switch engine was spotting cars. As soon as one was filled it was pushed down the siding and an empty was moved up to the chutes.

"The shippin' is goin' full blast," the Kid said to himself, his worst fears confirmed. "I knew we'd walk right into it!"

They drove into the vacant lot opposite the hotel. Isaiah gave the boy some instructions and went off at once to purchase a peddler's license. When he returned the platform was still up and the Kid was out of sight. The old man found him hiding in the wagon.

"The idea!" he roared, angrier than the boy had ever seen him. "Hiding in here like a scared rabbit! You lower the platform and start passing out the handbills as I told you! We didn't come this long piece just for the ride!"

The Kid sat there; he wasn't to be bullied. The prophet began to regret his temper. In a much milder tone he said, "I ran into the marshal down the street and we had a nice little chat. We won't have any difficulty with him."

Some of the defiance faded out of the boy's mouth.

"That may be the way it looks now," he observed thinly, "but if some puncher recognizes me the jig will be up; that badge toter will be Johnny on the spot to jug me."

Gran'pap shook his head to the contrary. "David, you don't have to worry for a minute! If some tipsy cowboy claims to know you, look a hole through him and pretend you never saw him before and leave the rest to me; I'll convince him he doesn't know you from Adam."

The Kid opened up the wagon and slipped into the red coat. Taking up his position at the sidewalk, he passed out the handbills for an hour. No one hailed him with a familiar shout of recognition. Trouble threatened from another direction, however. A little man, leaning heavily on a cane, hobbled up to the wagon.

"Whar's the old skinflint who runs this outfit?" he demanded irately. "I bin waitin' fer him to show his face in Lander agin!"

Isaiah was in the wagon. He stepped out at once.

"Thar yuh are!" the little man yelped. "I bought a bottle o' thet medicine o' yores, an' it ain't wuth the powder to blow it to hell, an' yuh know it! Either I'm gittin' my money back or I'm standin' right here tonight an' tellin' folks a thing or two!"

The prophet had handled disgruntled customers before. "My friend, I'll be glad to refund your money. That's the way I do business: satisfaction guaranteed, or return the empty bottle and get your money back. You took the Golden Elixir according to the directions?"

"I shore did! Took every drop of it. Thar's more good in two fingers of rye, I kin tell yuh!"

Isaiah led him around to the front of the wagon and sat down with him. The Kid couldn't catch what they were saying, but the conversation seemed to have taken a friendly turn. After the little man had hobbled away Gran'pap came around to the sidewalk.

"I told you to expect somethin' like that," said the Kid.

Isaiah smiled contentedly. "I fixed him up. He'll be on hand tonight to give a rip-snorting testimonial for the elixir. I promised him a couple of dollars. It'll be worth it."

The Kid had supper out of the way before night fell. Gran'pap hung up the lamps. The street was busier than it had been all afternoon; men were trooping in and out of the saloons. Across the way, at the hotel, there wasn't space enough on the porch to accommodate the crowd, and it overflowed to the sidewalk. Almost without exception they were rangemen, either cowboys or owners. Several trail herds were being held on the bed grounds outside of town, awaiting their turn at the shipping pens. They sent in reinforcements to join the crowd. It made the old man beam.

"We struck it just right," he told himself. "Most of them have got their wages in their pocket."

He was not discounting the possibility that someone might recognize the boy. On his own account he was every bit as much concerned about it as the Kid, but for an entirely different reason. His strongest hold on David was the myth that he was wanted. Isaiah knew that story would be exploded the minute the lad got into conversation with an old acquaintance. Once he learned the truth, he would be off; nothing would induce him to stay with the wagon.

"I'll keep my eyes open tonight," he said to himself. "It's altogether unlikely that anything will come of it."

He lit the lamps and told the boy to push the organ into position. A couple of men were passing. One of them was Kenny Singleton, a Double Diamond rider. Singleton glanced at the boy in the red coat and hurried on with his friend to disappear in the saloon.

The Kid licked his dry lips and threw off his trance. "If Double Diamond is in Lander," he thought, "that's gettin' close to home!"

Double Diamond range lay a few miles south of Medicine Flat.

Gran'pap had begun to beat a tambourine to attract attention and announce that the show was about to begin. Men started strolling over from the hotel. In a few minutes a crowd of fifty or more was gathered about the wagon. There was the usual sprinkling of women in it and, in addition, a score of boys of assorted ages. The little man with the cane pressed close to the platform.

The Kid played "Camptown Races" and several lively hoe-downs. It was then time for his first song. Isaiah introduced him as "that great little artist with the golden voice." He sat down at the organ to play the accompaniment and nodded for David to step forward.

The crowd greeted the Kid with a round of applause. His repertoire had grown remarkably since his last appearance in Lander and now included a number of popular cowboy ballads. He began with "Little Joe, the Wrangler" and received an ovation from the audience. He sang "Lorena" for them, and "Buffalo Gals."

"Buffalo gals, will you come out tonight,
come out tonight, come out tonight,
Buffalo gals, will you come out tonight
and dance by de light ob de moon?"

At the organ Isaiah smiled with a great satisfaction. Things were going fine! Remembering the spell "Come Where My Love Lies Dreaming" had cast over the crowd on the first visit to Lander, he had been showman enough to keep that for last.

It was still the Kid's best song, and he poured his heart into it. Halfway through there was an interruption. “Good grief, Kenny, it’s the Driftin’ Kid!” a man exclaimed excitedly. The crowd turned on him and told him to shut up.

The Kid found something familiar about the voice. He tried not to locate the owner of it. Eyes blank, his knees shaking, he continued with his song. Gran’pap was playing louder and louder.

The Kid finished and took several bows. Isaiah was on his feet in a flash, arms outstretched for attention. Out of the corner of his eye he saw a cowpuncher shouldering his way to the platform. The Kid saw the man too. It was Johnnie Hines, who had fought with Joe Trapnell and taken such an unmerciful beating!

“Hi, Kid!” Johnnie called when he reached the wagon. “You’re a sight for sore eyes! What yuh doin’ in that rig?”

The Kid gave him a stony stare that held no recognition and turned his back on him.

“Say, what’s the idea—” Johnnie started to demand.

“My friend, you’re interrupting the proceedings,” Isaiah told him firmly. “I appreciate your enthusiasm, but I’m afraid you’ve been sampling the wrong kind of medicine this evening.” The crowd understood this bit of humor and laughed uproariously. “This lad is my grandson; we’re from Tennessee. You are mistaking him for someone else.” Isaiah turned to David. “Do you know this man, son?”

The Kid shook his head.

Johnnie didn't know what to make of it. He had had a few drinks, but his imbibing was in nowise responsible for his befuddlement. Isaiah took an air with him that was both patient and indulgent.

"You see, my friend, how easy it is to be mistaken? If you will kindly step aside now we will continue with the program."

The crowd was with him and against Johnnie. "Pipe down, cowboy!" a raucous voice advised. There were similar mutterings from others. Johnnie had no more to say, but he planted himself at the edge of the platform, determined to stick there until the show was over. Isaiah ignored him and beckoned for the crowd to move in closer.

"I'm going to give you some scientific information regarding the human body—information your doctor won't give you, my friends! If he did you could cure yourself and he'd have to go out of business!"

The crowd tittered appreciatively. The Kid handed the pointer to the prophet and took his place at the iron stand from which the series of colored charts were suspended. He kept his eyes away from Johnnie. How long would it be, he wondered, before the marshal climbed up on the wagon to arrest him?

He listened to the old man's lecture with so

little interest that he had to be reminded several times to turn a leaf.

Isaiah's mind was busy as he talked. It was too late to waste any thought on regretting his decision to return to Lander. By the look of him, this pint-sized cowboy was going to be hard to handle. Who the man might be was immaterial; it was enough that he was one of David's old range acquaintances.

No fault was to be found with the way the boy had met the situation; David was a good little trouper. That he could continue to put up a bold front and convince the cowboy that they were strangers was expecting too much. Isaiah saw clearly that if disaster was to be averted, he, personally, must accomplish it.

Though he had a great talent for chicanery, no artful maneuver occurred to him that held any great promise of success. The best plan seemed to be to keep David in the wagon and make a hurried departure from Lander.

He quickly dismissed the thought that he could appeal to the town marshal for assistance if the man became obstreperous. The ice was already too thin for anything like that; he would have to take care of this pertinacious cowboy by himself.

The little man with the cane proved to be an excellent capper. He told the crowd that the first bottle of the Golden Elixir had almost cured the rheumatism that had plagued him for years. He purchased two bottles with the money Isaiah had provided for that purpose. It induced others to hand up their six bits, and for a few minutes business was brisk.

"Just a few bottles left, friends! Who'll be the next to have one?"

The prophet knew that the quickest and best way to disperse a street crowd was to give no more entertainment and keep on with the sales talk. It worked just as well in Lander as elsewhere.

He managed a few whispered words with the Kid. "Get everything inside," he ordered. "I'll keep on talking till they're all gone. You stay in the wagon; I'll hitch the mules and we'll pull out of here in a hurry!"

He extolled the merits of the elixir and kept importuning the remaining listeners to purchase a bottle until only a handful were left. They soon drifted away and only Johnnie Hines remained. Isaiah turned out the lights and told the boy to pull up the platform and bolt it from the inside.

"Say, Doc, I'll buy a bottle of that junk of yours if yuh'll just let me talk to yuh and the Kid," Johnnie offered.

"You're too late, my friend; we're through for the night. You'll have to catch us the next time we're in town."

Isaiah got down to the ground with greater agility than he was used to showing and started around the wagon to get the mules. Johnnie caught him by the arm.

"Just a minute, Doc! What's behind all this? Why yuh givin' me the brush-off? I know the Kid from away back. Why's he purtendin' he don't know me?"

"I'm sorry, my friend," the old man said with great severity. "My grandson ain't pretending nothing. You have him mixed up with someone else. You'll have to excuse me now; we have a long all-night drive to our next town."

Johnnie let him go and appeared to accept defeat. The prophet was no sooner out of sight, however, than Johnnie whipped out a knife and, climbing over a rear wheel, made a long slit in the tilt and scrambled inside.

"Johnnie, are you crazy, doin' that?" the Kid demanded in an excited whisper, his face pale in the feeble light of the lantern that hung from one of the bows.

"Then yuh do know me, Kid! I figgered yuh did! What was that stuff outside—purtendin' yuh didn't?"

"You ought to know without askin'!" was the scolding answer. "What do you want 'em to do—pick me up? Blabbin' out like that!"

"Pick yuh up for what, Kid?"

The boy shook his head pityingly. "You're as thick as Elmer used to be! You know I tried to help him get away. I been on the dodge for months. That's why I hooked up with Gran'pap. There's a warrant out on me."

"Who says there's a warrant out on yuh?" Johnnie was all ears now.

"Gran'pap, for one. He saw the notice tacked up in the post office in Thermopolis."

"He did, eh?" Johnnie whipped out. "By damn, I'm beginnin' to smell a rat! Yuh ain't wanted no more'n I be! The only party who's lookin' for yuh is Grady Roberts!"

Their voices had reached Isaiah, and he came piling into the wagon, eyes blazing, his long white hair and beard swirling about his head like an angry surf breaking on a rock-bound shore.

"Get out!" he shouted. "Get out of here this minute! Get out before I call the marshal!"

"Stop it, yuh ornery old crook!" Johnnie was bursting with outrage. "If the law is called, I'll be the one to do it! Makin' the Kid think he was wanted so yuh could use him for yore own ends! If I stepped across the street and told those boys what yuh've been up to, they'd tar and feather yuh and ride yuh out of town on a rail, old as yuh be!"

"You've got your facts twisted, mister!" the old man stormed. "I took the boy at his own word; he told me the law was after him!"

"What about the wanted notice yuh told him yuh saw in Thermopolis?"

"I said the description fitted him—that was all!"

"Yo're lyin' by the clock, yuh old snorter! Yuh didn't see no notice in Thermopolis. Yuh weren't even in the town or yuh'd know the post office burnt down this spring and they was handin' out the mail from the stage station."

Isaiah sat down heavily; he was trapped in his lie. "I thought I saw it in Thermopolis. It must have been somewhere else." His ruddy face was ashen. Why, oh, why, had he insisted on returning to Lander! "I—I tried to protect the boy. I thought that was what I was doing. He was in rags—half starved—when he came to me. Look at him now! Had he been my own flesh and blood I couldn't have treated him more kindly. Tell that to this man, David!"

"You treated me all right," the Kid acknowledged. "But you lied to me, Gran'pap, so I wouldn't pull away from you. You shouldn't-a done it."

Isaiah winced and sat there with a stricken look on his face; the boy had made life easy for him, brought in the money. He couldn't go on without him; he couldn't even bear to think of it.

"Don't be too hard on me, David," he pleaded. "Don't leave me! We'll make a fresh start. There'll be more money in it for you. I'll make up for the wrong I did you."

"Kid, are yuh goin' to let him git around yuh with that line of talk?" Johnnie demanded caustically. "The old son of a gun will trim yuh one way or another!"

"You like the life on the wagon, David," the prophet continued. "If you go back to range work you'll get slapped around like you did before, and you'll always be looking for another job. This job is steady, David; you'll never have to worry about where the next meal is coming from. And there'll be the crowds, the excitement, the applause, and the singing and music! Don't let this cowboy stampede you into making a mistake."

The Kid stood there silent, tight-lipped, holding his decision in abeyance. It was true that it was an easy life on the wagon. And it certainly made you feel good to stand up before a street-corner crowd and have the cheers and applause ringing in your ears. Believing the law was after him had kept him from enjoying the full thrill of those moments. That wouldn't be the case in the future; if he went on with Gran'pap he could face an audience unafraid. But there were other considerations: there was the debt he owed Elmer, and there was Grady. It left him no choice.

"I'm goin' to leave you, Gran'pap," he said simply. "Give me the money I got comin' and we'll call it quits."

Isaiah winced. The presence of this troublesome cowboy left him no alternative but to pay up. He had fallen on evil days indeed.

"You'll regret your decision, David!" he

protested. "You'll regret it! I know what's behind it. For you to go back to your old stamping ground with the idea that you can bring that deputy sheriff to account for killing Elmer is absolute folly. It will lead you into trouble as sure as you're standing there. You forget that you're only a boy. If you won't take my advice, perhaps you'll listen to your friend." His attention shifted to Johnnie. "You know the party I'm referring to—Daggett, I think his name is."

Johnnie nodded. "I know him." He flicked a surprised glance at the boy. "Kid, yuh ain't thinkin' of tanglin' with Chalk?"

"I'm goin' to let folks know what a rat he is! He didn't have to kill Elmer. Shootin' down an unarmed man who didn't have a chance of gettin' away ain't goin' to be overlooked if I can help it!"

This was the first time Johnnie had heard the details of what had occurred that morning on the Stinking Water. It differed greatly from the account Daggett had given.

"This old duffer's got it right," said Johnnie. "Don't yuh go back lookin' for trouble with Chalk. Keep yore lip buttoned till yuh've had a talk with Grady, and do exactly as he tells yuh. He's got Mr. Daggett on the skids."

"What do you mean?" the Kid demanded eagerly.

"It's a long story. Hoke Tuller's runnin' for

sheriff agin. Grady got about a hundred of us to sign a petition sayin' we wouldn't support Hoke unless he guaranteed us he wouldn't reappoint Daggett."

"And Hoke agreed to it?"

"Hunh! He had to if he wanted to git elected. You'll find Grady at Quarter Moon. He's ramroddin' the spread for Ruxton."

This was wonderful news. Wild horses could not have held the boy back now.

"You mean he's gone to Quarter Moon as foreman?"

Johnnie nodded. "Come on, Gran'pap, give him his money. How much yuh got comin', Kid?"

"Two dollars a week since the first of May comes to about forty-four, I figure."

"And he made plenty off yuh," Johnnie remarked sourly. "Hand him fifty bucks, Gran'pap, and we'll call it square."

Isaiah flatly rejected the proposition; it was bad enough to have to part with forty-four dollars.

"I fed and clothed him, I'll have you remember! The outfit he's wearing belongs to me!"

"You said it was mine when you give it to me," the Kid spoke up.

"Don't worry," Johnnie told him. "It's yores. Count out his wages, Gran'pap, and we'll be on our way. Is there anythin' else around here that belongs to yuh, Kid?"

"My saddle and bridle—and my gun."

"Gun? What yuh doin' with a gun?"

"I found it."

"Wal, gather up yore stuff and give me the gun. I'll fetch it up to Grady and he can keep it for yuh; yuh don't need a gun."

Isaiah opened his tin box and counted out the forty-four dollars with a trembling hand. He had encountered adversity many times but had never been left so crushed and helpless.

The Kid bore him no enmity. In fact, there was only pity and a deep understanding of the old man in his heart as he gazed at him. He knew he was going to miss Isaiah.

The gold-braided red coat caught his eye. He had always felt so proud to wear it. He ran his hand over it in farewell. Johnnie had stepped down from the wagon. The Kid handed him his saddle.

"Come on!" Johnnie urged.

The Kid held back and turned to Isaiah. "I'll be goin', I reckon," he got out, a catch in his voice. "You take good care of Jeptha and Japtha and don't let 'em get run down the way they was when I joined up with you . . . So long, Gran'pap!"

The prophet just sat there, head bowed.

Johnnie hurried the Kid across town to the Double Diamond wagon and provided him with a blanket.

"We'll be through loadin' about the middle of

the mornin'," said Johnnie. "It won't be no later than noon when we pull out of Lander for the ranch. It'll give yuh a ride almost all the way up."

The Kid carried his blanket out on the flat, but he could not go to sleep. As he lay there he heard the familiar creaking of a wagon. He sat up stiffly, his heart pounding, and saw it moving slowly along the road that ran to Casper. Isaiah sat hunched over on the seat, looking neither to right nor left.

The Kid watched the wagon with blurred eyes until it disappeared from view. "Gee, I dunno—he's an old fake and he lied to me—but I hope he does all right in Casper," he murmured, his voice tremulous and uncertain.

9

Kenny Singleton was one of several in Double Diamond's trail crew who were surprised to learn that the boy they had heard singing with the medicine show was the Drifting Kid.

"Reckon we failed to spot you because none of us ever figgered you'd be comin' at us as a medicine-show grifter," Kenny said, summing it up for himself and the others. "How long was you with that outfit?"

"All summer. We were all the way out to Idaho and Nevada."

They were camped for the night at Mud Springs, thirty miles north of Lander. The Kid was the center of attention as the crew relaxed around the fire. He was easily the most widely traveled man among them, and he had been living a life that their imaginations invested with glamour.

"Tell the boys about yore mix-up with Painless Peters," Johnnie urged. "Tell it just like yuh told me."

The Kid related the incident. It opened the door, and he spoke freely of his experiences on the wagon with Isaiah. The attention he got made him feel important; in the old days no one had ever given him any consideration.

Someone mentioned the killing of Joe Trapnell. The Kid didn't need Johnnie's warning wink to put him on guard; he didn't propose to say anything about Trapnell or Elmer.

Ab Byers got his guitar from the chuck wagon and began strumming it. "How about givin' us a song, Kid? One of those yuh sang last evenin'. That 'Come Where My Love Lies Dreamin'' is an awful purty one."

The Kid shook his head. "I don't feel like singin' tonight, Ab. It's nice just to hear you play. When I was with the show I often wished I could play the guitar."

"Stay away from the gitar, Kid," Ab declared with a grin. "Gitar playin' has been the ruin of more cowboys than whisky. Jest look at me and yuh can see what I mean."

It was one of Ab's favorite jokes.

The Kid had some questions. Almost without exception they concerned Grady Roberts.

"I sure hope I can catch on at Quarter Moon," he told Johnnie. "That's a fine spread; Lee Ruxton ain't hirin' and firin' men spring and fall like Flat Iron. If you get a job with him you're all set."

"Yeh," Johnnie agreed. "Guess he was glad to git Grady back. I got it purty straight that he was all set to make him foreman 'way back when that trouble came up over Steve Ennis. Grady will shore be surprised to see yuh, Kid."

"Reckon he will," the boy said, gazing into the fire. "He told me he'd be around if I ever came back. Most likely I'll find him out on the range; Quarter Moon must be makin' its gather."

"I dunno; they ship awful late. We'll hit the house sometime tomorrow afternoon. That'll leave yuh about twelve miles to go. I'll loan yuh a bronc out of my string. That'll beat hoofin' it."

The following afternoon the Kid found himself in the saddle again. Somehow the world looked different when surveyed from the back of a good bronc. In his eagerness to see Grady, thoughts of old Isaiah receded from his mind.

In the old days he had never given a thought to his appearance. Life on the wagon had changed all that and he had spent some time brushing his clothes and polishing his boots for the reunion with Grady.

From the road, in passing, he had observed the house and other buildings on Lee Ruxton's Quarter Moon ranch many times. The house was the finest in this corner of Wyoming. Barns, the crew's quarters, saddle shed, blacksmith shop, and several other small frame structures were so situated as to frame the ranch yard. They had always looked neat and in good repair.

The Kid never had had any business at Quarter

Moon and didn't know his way around. When he rode in an hour before dark he went to the house and left his bronc at the hitch rail. He knew Lee Ruxton—a tall, thin man, a little stooped—by sight, having seen him many times in Medicine Flat.

An unroofed gallery ran down the length of the front of the house. The Kid mounted the steps and started looking for Ruxton's office. The yard was deserted and it led him to conclude that Quarter Moon's roundup was on. At the end of the gallery a small sign above an open door bore the single word, "Office."

A girl about his own age stepped out before he reached the door. They were mutually surprised to find themselves facing each other.

"I didn't hear you ride in," she said. She had copper-red hair that fell to her shoulders. The Kid wasn't aware whether she was pretty or not; he never noticed such things. He recalled vaguely that Ruxton had a daughter who had been away to school for years and took it for granted that this red-haired girl was she.

"I'm lookin' for Grady Roberts, miss," he said, removing his black Stetson as he addressed her and trying not to appear self-conscious. He had learned his manners with old Isaiah.

"Everybody's out on the east range," she told him. "Father and Grady will be in this evening. I'm Paula Ruxton." She gave the Kid a warm, friendly smile, regarding him the while with eyes that were frankly curious. "Could you be the boy Grady calls the Drifting Kid?"

The Kid nodded, too startled to pretend otherwise. "Reckon I'll wait for him if you think he'll be in. I'll just go over to the bunkhouse and hang around till he shows up. Sorry I bothered you, Miss Ruxton," he added apologetically.

"It wasn't any bother," said Paula. "Grady has told me all about you. That little white cottage is his. I don't believe he is expecting you."

"Reckon not," the Kid replied. "I been away some time . . . I'll thank you again."

"You could wait here on the gallery," Paula suggested. "You might find it more comfortable."

The Kid was definitely embarrassed by now and wanted to flee, but when she offered him a chair he took it. To his dismay she sat down with him.

Paula made the conversation. She had no difficulty in drawing him out. In fact, the Kid was putty in her hands. Before he realized it, she had him feeling at ease.

"That must have been loads of fun, traveling with a medicine show," she told him. "I've been locked up in a convent for years. Boys have all the best of it."

"We didn't always sell medicine," said the Kid. "You might say the Golden Elixir was just our side line; salvation was Gran'pap's long suit;

when he really got goin' he could sling gospel better'n anybody I ever heard."

There was an imp of deviltry in Paula, and old Isaiah's sacrilegious charlatanry amused rather than shocked her. Her green eyes flashed with merriment. "I almost wish I were back at St. Margaret's so I could tell Sister Mary Rose. She'd be horrified!"

With a guile that fooled the Kid completely, she got him to expand on his professional activities on the wagon. The crowds had always made a big fuss over his singing, he admitted without too much reluctance. He named towns where they would have had him singing all night if he hadn't called a halt. "One night out in Idaho, in one of the minin' towns, they threw money at me," he informed her, not aware of where all this was leading him. "I picked up over two dollars."

"It's wonderful to be able to sing like that," Paula said innocently. "Or are you just making up all of this?"

"No," the Kid averred stoutly. "I don't mean to throw bouquets at myself, but when you're in the singin' business you got to be purty good."

"I'm dying to hear you," said Paula. "I can't sing a note. I do play the piano. At school everybody said I was a good accompanist. If I play will you sing a song for me?"

The Kid shook his head. He felt like kicking

himself for walking into her trap. “Some other time, maybe,” he begged off.

Paula laughed, and he caught a note of mockery. “I thought you were fooling me,” she said.

The Kid longed to impress her, but even though his veracity was being questioned now, he refused to oblige. He didn’t like being tricked; then, too, he didn’t believe in giving in to girls. That was how they got the whip hand over you.

He had observed girls on the ranches where he had worked. Mrs. Button’s niece had come up from Cheyenne one year to spend her vacation at 7 Bar and had ruined the summer for him. But he had never known a girl quite like Paula Ruxton, he admitted. She didn’t pretend to be shy and half scared to death when she talked to you, the way most girls did. And there wasn’t anything uppish about her, even if she had been away to school and her father one of the richest men in this part of Wyoming. For all her money, she was dressed in a checkered cotton shirt and Levi’s. Only her boots were expensive.

“Well, if you won’t sing, you won’t,” she said. “I guess you know something about horses—good horses, I mean.”

“A little bit,” the Kid replied, making sure he didn’t put himself out on the end of the limb a second time.

“I mean hot-blooded horses—thoroughbreds,” Paula explained.

"That's what I thought you meant. I've done a little ridin' for Cleve Taylor. I rode against one of your dad's horses in Cody." He could have said he won that race.

"That must have been Star Gazer," said Paula. "We didn't do so well with him. We've got a two-year-old coming along that looks a lot better. We call him Blue Rocket. He belongs to me and he's a beauty. Dad bought him in California. He's only been on the ranch a week or two. I'll show him to you in the morning."

"I don't know that I'll be around," he replied.

Paula looked up, surprised. "Aren't you going to strike Grady for a job?"

"No, I just dropped by to say hello."

This was the Kid's pride speaking. He didn't want her to think he had any intention of trading on his friendship with her father's foreman. He wouldn't let Grady think that either; if a job was offered him he'd grab it, but he wasn't asking for one.

The Kid had not fully recovered from her directness when she startled him again.

"If you don't ask him I shall—or I'll speak to Dad. That's if you're open for a job. You could help me with Blue Rocket if you liked. I want to race him next fall. It's pretty hard to get a horse ready when you have to work him alone . . . I guess we'd get along all right if you didn't mind me getting up on my ear now and then; I know some words I didn't learn at the convent."

The Kid could not have dreamed up a more pleasing prospect for himself. And yet he felt it incumbent on him not to appear too eager to accept.

"I dunno," he declared thoughtfully. "It might be all right. If Grady or your father make me a proposition I'll consider it."

Paula felt rebuffed at his lack of appreciation and gave up trying to break through his reserve. The offer she had made him wasn't to be had just for the asking; her father let her have her way in many things, but he could say no, too.

"Thank you for agreeing to think it over, at least," she said, intending by her careless tone to let him know how unimportant the matter was. "You'll undoubtedly find something that will suit you better," she added, getting to her feet. "I'll have to go in and get out of these overalls for dinner; I promised Dad I'd doll up a little for him if he'd come in."

She excused herself and left the Kid sitting there, feeling he had been put in his proper place. He built a cigarette with great care and smoked it thoughtfully. No question about it, he concluded after some lengthy deliberation, Paula Ruxton knew how to twist you around her finger.

"In no time at all she'd be bossin' the life out of me," he told himself. "But she ain't no sissy." This was a great compliment. "If she can get her old man to tell Grady to take me on, it'll be okay with me!"

Someone went through the house, lighting the lamps. What daylight there was left was fading quickly now. The Kid had been watching the range to the east for some sign of Grady and Ruxton. He was about ready to give up when he saw two riders moving toward the yard at a leisurely pace. He took it for granted that one of them was Roberts, and he moved his borrowed bronc across the yard to the foreman's cottage and perched himself on the steps.

In a few minutes he heard the two men turn their mounts into the horse corral. One of them walked to the house; the other, tall and wide of shoulder, headed for the cottage.

"It's Grady!" the Kid exclaimed softly. "I'd know him a mile!"

Roberts noticed the bronc tethered at the rail in front of the cottage, but the porch steps were dark and he didn't see the Kid.

"Hi ya, Grady!" the latter called.

"Who's there?" was the quick question.

The Kid chuckled. "Bet you couldn't guess!"

Grady's step lengthened and, peering through the deep twilight, he recognized his visitor. "You! The Kid!" he exclaimed, his voice warm and welcoming. "This *is* a surprise!"

The tall man clapped his hands on the boy's shoulders and looked him over carefully.

"I was beginning to think I'd never be seeing you again," he said. "Where are you from now? And where have you been?"

"I been a lot of places." The Kid grinned, his heart pounding happily. "I got so much to tell you I can't give it to you all at once . . . You haven't changed a bit, Grady! I hear things have been breakin' good for you."

"Yes, they have—much better than I deserved," was the modest answer. "You're looking fine, Kid—and prosperous too. A new suit—"

"Yeh, and I've got a little bank roll in my pocket. I didn't come back broke."

"Well, let's go in," said Roberts. "I'll strike a light and we can clean up a little and have something to eat. The boss has a Chink who cooks for the family. I eat with the crew. We have our own dining room and cook. He's out with the wagon right now. But we can go down to the kitchen and rustle up something for ourselves. The boss would ask us over if he thought I had a friend with me. There's only he and his daughter in the family."

"I met his daughter," the Kid observed.

"Did you? How long have you been here?"

"I rode in about an hour ago. She sat down on the gallery with me. Spotted me right off and asked me if I was the Driftin' Kid she'd heard you speak of."

Roberts laughed quietly. "I've often talked

about you to Paula. She's a fine kid, a real straight-shooter. I sometimes think she must have just missed being a boy. Do you like her?"

"She's all right—for a girl."

"Still down on girls, eh? You're getting along to the time when you're going to find them mighty interesting, Kid."

He opened the door and they stepped inside.

"Is that your bronc at the rail?" Grady asked.

"No, I got the loan of it from Johnnie Hines. I came up from Lander with the Double Diamond crew. I never would have taken a chance on comin' back if it hadn't been for Johnnie. I thought the law was lookin' for me. He set me straight about it." The Kid was sizing up Grady's quarters. "They certainly treat you right on this spread—fixin' you up nice and comfortable like this."

"It's a good outfit," said Grady, busy at the washstand. "They don't come any better. Did Johnnie tell you I had been looking for you?"

"He told me. Said you'd been up to Billings last month."

"They had a Hereford stock show up there," the tall man explained. "I went up with the boss. We bought two prize bulls. I looked around for you. We came back through Cody and stayed there overnight. I inquired about you there. It was tough the way things turned out for Elmer. The two of you must have parted company before they caught up with him. Link Hinchman was with Daggett. I talked to him afterward. He told me they hadn't seen anything of you . . . Do you want to wash up a little? I'll lay out a towel for you."

"So one of those gents was Link Hinchman, eh?" the Kid muttered tensely. He pulled off his coat and rolled up his shirt sleeves. "I'm glad to know it! Maybe he was tellin' the truth, and maybe he wasn't; I was on the Stinking Water that mornin'. I saw what they handed Elmer. Daggett didn't give him no more chance than he and Trapnell gave Steve."

Roberts's face whipped hard and flat. "You actually saw it, Kid?"

"I sure did! I was up on the ridge, across the river from 'em. Daggett had two men ridin' with him. Daggett was closest. Elmer didn't have a chance of gettin' away. The big horse he took from camp had gone lame, and he was ridin' my little bronc. You know he wasn't worth shucks as a rider. Besides, he was too big and heavy for that pony. He musta known the jig was up. I could see his knees and elbows flappin' as he tried to get a little more speed out of the pony."

"Did he have a gun?" Grady asked.

"Course he didn't! Daggett could see that; he was so close that he could have pulled Elmer out of the saddle in another couple minutes. But the dirty rat whips up his rifle and blazes away at him! The first shot went wide; the second finished Elmer. I reckon he was dead before he hit the ground."

Roberts stood there, grim and tight-lipped. The Kid believed he read the man's thought: there was a parallel between the slaying of Steve Ennis and Elmer. There had been no witness to testify as to how Steve was rubbed out. None was necessary now.

"If I'd ever needed any proof to convince me that they murdered Steve, this would be it, Kid! It knocks the last shred of doubt out of it." He stood there, silent and thoughtful for a moment. When he continued his mood was more sober than ever. "I don't want you to get me wrong, Kid, but I'm sorry you came back."

"What?" the boy exclaimed, aghast. "You don't mean that, Grady!"

"Yes, I do, Kid, and I'm thinking only of your end of it. You've got too much on Daggett for your own safety. When what you've just told me reaches his ears, he'll realize in a second that he's got to run you out of this country or shut your mouth in some way. Have you talked with anyone else?"

"Just Johnnie. He advised me to keep still about it until I got to you. He wouldn't have said that if he was goin' to go blabbin' everythin' I said."

"He won't mean to, Kid, but he'll talk, and it'll get to Daggett. In two or three days he'll know you're back and all about what you've got on him. If I had run into you in Lander and heard your story I'd have done everything I could to stop you from coming back. You understand why I say that?"

The Kid, a picture of despair, nodded tragically. "Does that mean you're goin' to send me away, Grady? You can't do that! All the time I been away I've been achin' to get back here with you. I was travelin' with a wagon show—singin', playin' the organ and mouth harp, and doin' fine. The old gent who owned the outfit was a crook and he lied somethin' awful to me, but it was nice work. I threw it up just as soon as I found out the law didn't want me. I figured if the two of us was together we could take care of Chalk Daggett. Elmer got into trouble on my account and got killed for it. I know what I owe him, and it's got to be taken care of. If it means washin' dishes again and swampin' out bunkhouses, well, I ain't too good for it. I coulda said it was none of my business and gone on with the show, but I wouldn't have had no use for myself."

Roberts was moved by the boy's sense of integrity and confidence in him. Characteristically he gave little sign of it. He said, "I should be the last one in the world to find fault with your loyalty to Elmer. Just the same, Kid, the smartest thing I could do would be to pack you off in the morning and tell you to locate that barnstorming wagon and stick with it. But I'm not going to do it—not for the present, at least. If you're going to be around I want you to be where I can keep my eye on you. That'll mean sticking close to the ranch."

The Kid brightened perceptibly. "Does that mean you're offerin' me a job?" He tried to make the question sound casual.

"Not exactly a job," said Grady. "But you can earn your keep until the roundup is over and we have our beef started for Lander. There's very little hiring and firing on this spread, Kid. The crew is bigger now than we really need, but that's Lee Ruxton's way: he keeps the men on the year around, and when one of them gets too old for riding he makes a job for him that will keep him busy . . . By the way, did Johnnie tell you that Daggett will be out of the sheriff's office after election?"

"Yeh, he told me you got up the petition," the Kid answered out of his preoccupation. He had counted heavily on Grady being able to find a job for him.

"Daggett figured that Tuller wouldn't run again and that would give him a chance to be put up. Now he knows he won't even be deputy sheriff."

"I bet that slayed him!" the Kid muttered.

"He isn't saying much. I don't know what's behind it—unless he figures that if he plays his cards right Tuller will go back on his word after the votes are counted and reappoint him in spite of everything."

"Is there any chance that old Hoke will double-cross you, Grady?"

"I don't think so, but if that's what Daggett is counting on, he'll realize when your story gets to him that he's finished unless he stops you. That's what I mean, Kid, when I say I wish you hadn't come back. Daggett is dangerous enough even when things are breaking his way; there's no telling what he'll do when he gets desperate . . . Finish cleaning up, and we'll get ourselves some supper."

As they started down the yard a few minutes later Ruxton called to Roberts from the gallery. "Grady, you and the boy have dinner with us! There's nobody in the kitchen to take care of you!"

Roberts was about to beg off, when the Kid brought the heel of his boot down on the tall man's toes in an unmistakable bid for him to accept the invitation. Roberts amended his answer and called back that they would be pleased to come over.

The tall man flashed a glance at the Kid that held a mild surprise; the change in the boy was greater than he had supposed. He was growing up; learning how to assert himself.

"I thought you didn't like girls," Grady said banteringly.

"Hunh! Who said anythin' about girls? You tell me you can't take me on. Maybe Ruxton can. He's the boss of this outfit, ain't he?"

Roberts laughed quietly. "He's supposed to be, but I wonder sometimes if he doesn't get his orders too."

10

Roberts smiled to himself as he sat back and marveled at the ease with which the Kid held his own with Paula Ruxton and her father. He knew the boy had a great sense of pride and dignity, but to find him so unself-conscious and forthright made the tall man realize how completely unaware the lad was of any social barrier between himself and those who were better placed.

Ruxton noted it, too, and found it refreshing. Having come up the hard way and put Quarter Moon together by his own efforts and made himself a rich man had not produced the faintest trace of snobbery in him. The few pretensions he allowed himself were on Paula's account; he was ambitious for her. She was as high-spirited as a thoroughbred, and fully as unpredictable. But time would take care of that, he felt. Young as she was, she was giving promise of becoming a beautiful young woman, like her dead mother in many ways, but possessing a vitality that she got from him. It pleased him to see her so sure of herself as she played the lady with the boy.

Paula was delighted to discover that Grady, as

well as her father, had not heard anything about Isaiah. Under her guidance the Kid retold the story of his days on the wagon as she had heard it that afternoon on the gallery. With the additions that she wormed out of him, they were at the table for half an hour after they finished dinner.

"Don't you miss Gran'pap and the wagon?" Paula asked, her eyes bright and excited. "And that red coat with the gold braid! It must have been wonderful!"

"Oh, I dunno," the Kid declared, shy for the first time with her. "I reckon it wasn't so much. It made you feel important in little towns like Powder City and Lander; it wouldn't have amounted to anythin' in Omaha or Chicago or any of them big places. As for bein' on the wagon—it was a free-and-easy life. But I wouldn't have stuck with Gran'pap for long; I'd have got to a big city and tried my luck. There wouldn't have been no chance of that with him; whenever I mentioned it he always said it was better to be a big frog in a small puddle than nobody in a big one. That might have been all right for him, but not for me; I want to get ahead and make somethin' of myself."

Ruxton nodded encouragingly. "You're right, my boy; you'll never know what you can do unless you try. Suppose you and Paula step into the parlor and let us hear what kind of a singer you are."

The Kid didn't hang back. Paula led him to the piano, where they could not be observed from the dinner table. The surroundings impressed the boy; he had never seen such an elegantly appointed room. He took it in stride. Paula's flashing eyes produced a mild confusion in him, however, that was not so easily mastered.

"Sing 'Lorena' for them," she urged, running her fingers over the keys. "It's Dad's favorite."

"Did you say anythin' to him about takin' me on?" the Kid inquired.

Paula laughed tantalizingly. "Wouldn't you like to know?"

"Maybe it doesn't matter," he replied soberly. "Grady says I shouldn't have come back. He's afraid Chalk Daggett will make trouble for me. You wouldn't understand."

"Wouldn't I?" Paula challenged. "I know more about Chalk Daggett than you think. He knows he isn't welcome here. You don't have to worry about that man, David; Dad will see to that."

"Then you *have* said somethin' to him about me?"

Paula nodded and continued playing.

"What was it—yes or no?" the Kid asked.

"He promised to speak to Grady. Sing now or they'll be wondering what we're up to!"

The plaintive melody was well suited for the boy's voice. Never in his days on the wagon had he sung "Lorena" with more feeling or a truer sense of tone. Grady and Ruxton were pleasantly surprised. Paula joined in their applause.

"That was beautiful, Daddy!" she called.

"Yes, it was! It was fine! Let's have some more!" To Roberts, Ruxton said, "Thank God he doesn't sing through his nose! His voice is as true as a bell. Paula's mother would have appreciated it. She had a trained voice; her folks spent a fortune on it, and then I had to bring her out to Wyoming to sing to the coyotes!" He shook his head regretfully. "I've often thought how unfair it was to her."

Having such a friendly and enthusiastic audience, the Kid outdid himself. He had sung half a dozen songs when Ruxton came to the parlor door. "Grady and I are going to step around to the office," he said. "We have a little business to talk over. I guess the two of you can amuse yourselves."

Roberts knew of no business they had to discuss other than the morrow's work. He was surprised, therefore, to discover that it concerned the Kid. Ruxton asked many questions about the boy's background as his foreman knew it. He was especially interested in the trouble at Camp Number 3 that had led up to the Kid's flight with Elmer and what had taken place that morning on the Stinking Water.

"I wish I could do something for him," Grady said at the end. "I mean—see that he gets a chance. I don't believe there's a wrong bone in his body."

"It's easy to see that he idolizes you," Ruxton declared. "You can't take it away from him, Grady; he's got the instincts of a gentleman. I've always shared your opinion of Chalk Daggett. I'm more convinced now than ever that he's got to go. We can't keep him from learning that the boy is back."

"No, he'll hear the whole story," Roberts agreed, "and charge it up to my account, no doubt; he holds me responsible for all his difficulties. That's the way I want it; he knows that any time he wants to come looking for satisfaction he can have it. But I don't want him to take it out on the Kid."

Ruxton leaned back in his chair and studied his cigar thoughtfully and soberly.

"You're bitter, Grady—and with good reason. I know Daggett is a blackleg, but for the life of me I can't see how he could hope to improve his position by going after the boy. There's so much feeling against him right now that if he tried anything like that it would raise such a stink that Hoke would have to get rid of him at once. And it could very easily cost Daggett more than his job . . . I wish I had known about this several months ago."

Ruxton had always kept clear of county politics, but he had an important voice in who was nominated and elected to the various offices. He had consistently backed Hoke Tuller. Roberts was surprised, therefore, to have him reverse himself at this late date. Ruxton spoke frankly.

"No one wants to hurt old Hoke's feelings; he served us well in the past. But it has become plainer every day that he's outlived his usefulness. He's been letting his authority slip through his fingers into Daggett's hands for a long time. He's come to depend on him so much that he thinks he can't run the office without him."

"The evidence has been there for you to see for a long time, Mr. Ruxton." Roberts's tone was as blunt as his words. "Tuller never believed that trumped-up story about Steve. But he swallowed it. That was the tip-off as to who was running the sheriff's office."

"I know it," the cowman admitted readily. "I can see it clearly enough now. But hindsight never was worth a damn. There's still time to do something; the elections are a month away."

Roberts reminded him that Tuller's name would be on the ballot. In a county that was solidly Republican, that was equivalent to election.

"There's nothing to stop us from writing in a candidate's name on the ballot, Grady. The thing to do is to have a showdown with Hoke. His promise not to reappoint Daggett isn't enough; if he wants my support he'll have to kick him out now. I'll get word to Reb Corson, so the three of us can go in together and have it out with Hoke, and we'll take the boy along and let him tell all he knows. That'll be better all the way around than trying to keep it a secret. The lad will be safe that way. Once the cat is out of the bag, Daggett will realize it's too late to do anything about shutting him up."

The tall man gave the idea his hearty approval.

"I'd like it even better," he said, "if we could attend to it tomorrow. But there isn't any chance of that; we'll be busy until dark finishing off the cut, and come daylight, we'll be starting for Lander."

"We won't be gone over five days. The boy will be all right here until we get back. Homer and three or four of the older hands will be around to look after things."

"I guess that's true," said Roberts, "though I had thought some of taking the Kid along with me."

Ruxton shook his head and smiled mysteriously. "I'm afraid that wouldn't work out, Grady, and leave me any peace of mind. I've been instructed to give David a job."

"Paula?" Roberts queried with a smile.

"Paula," said her father. "I don't know how it will work out, but she is full of ambitious plans about what they can do with Blue Rocket. I promised her I would recondition the quarter-mile track I laid out when I was racing Star Gazer. She's in dead earnest about this, Grady."

"I imagine she is," Roberts declared, mentally trying to fit the Kid into the circumstances. "She's crazy about the colt, and she seems to know what she's doing. The Kid has a way with horses. I don't know how well he can ride."

"He can ride, I assure you," Ruxton said with a chuckle. "Cleve Taylor had him up on one of his horses at Cody two years ago, and he made Star Gazer look pretty bad . . . I hardly know what to offer the boy. Is ten a month enough?"

"That's plenty. And you'll have to keep him busy or he won't think he's earning it. Let him get the idea that any part of it's charity, and he'll be gone."

"I'll leave it to you to keep him busy," the owner of Quarter Moon said brusquely. "You make him understand he takes his orders from you; I don't want Paula to get the idea that she's his boss. Suppose you bring him in and we'll see what he has to say about it."

Roberts found the Kid and Paula seated on the parlor floor playing stud poker. "Well, this is a fine note!" he exclaimed with mock severity. "Who suggested this?"

"I did," said Paula. "I wish we were playing for money. I'd have trimmed him good!"

"No doubt—with your cards," Roberts remarked, holding a straight face. "It looks like the same marked deck you used on your father and me one evening."

"Daggone, I wondered!" the Kid burst out. "I couldn't win a pot!"

Paula gathered up the cards and scrambled to her feet. "Grady, you can be a terrible stick when you want to!" She pouted. "A person can't get away with anything when you're around!"

"No?" he queried mockingly. "You seem to be doing all right . . . Come on, Kid! Mr. Ruxton wants to talk to you."

Shadow turned to sunshine in Paula and she threw her arms about Roberts and hugged him. "Is it all right, Grady?" she cried. "Did he say yes?"

The tall man gave her a cold eye. "Young woman, I haven't the slightest idea of what you're referring to. Your father wants to see the Kid, that's all."

"Grady, stop teasing me!" Paula protested. "Do you have to be so ornery? . . . I'm going in with you."

"You are not," he said firmly, and for all the laughter in his eyes, she knew he meant it.

The Kid didn't quite know how to take all this nonsense and banter. Paula caught him regarding her with a puzzled frown.

"Go on!" she urged. "And don't look so scared, David!"

The Kid said nothing, but he gave her a glance that was calculated to take her down a peg or two. Squaring his shoulders, he marched out with Roberts.

Ruxton looked up from some papers on his desk and invited the boy to take a chair. "I've been talking things over with Grady," he said. "I wonder if you'd be interested in going to work for Quarter Moon."

It came so quickly that it took the Kid by surprise, and he blurted out an eager "I sure would, Mr. Ruxton!" before he caught himself. "That is," he amended, "if you want to make me a proposition I'll be glad to consider it."

Ruxton outlined his "proposition" and filled in some of the details.

"Your mornings will be pretty well taken up with working out Blue Rocket," he continued. "You'll take your orders from Grady; he'll arrange the afternoon work for you. I'll start you off at ten dollars a month and I'll expect you to earn it. How does it strike you?"

"It sounds so good I can't believe it's happenin' to me," the Kid declared, all his pretenses forgotten. "I'll sure work my fingers off for you!" He beamed at Grady. "You won't have any reason to be sorry you recommended me."

"I haven't any doubt about that," Roberts assured him, the happiness mirrored on the boy's face giving him an emotional tug. "If I have to bear down on you a little now and then, I know you can take it."

"David, I hope you haven't forgotten how to ride," said Ruxton.

"I don't believe I have, sir. I may be a little heavier than I was when I was ridin' for Taylor, but I can work that off. The horse I beat you with in Cody was a green colt when I first got hold of him. It's slow work bringin' one along; you can't crowd 'em too much."

Paula's father nodded. "That's right; it takes a lot of patience. I'm going to depend on you to see that Paula doesn't let her enthusiasm run away with her. I've got a neat little bronc that can step three furlongs in better than forty-two seconds. Blue Rocket will work out all right with him. You'll find me an early-morning railbird when you get around to running him against a watch."

The Kid was literally walking on air: Grady and he were going to be together! Between them they'd find a way to avenge Elmer and Steve. But that wasn't all. He was going to be anchored somewhere at last—have a chance! Security would have been a better word for it. That was what he really had been seeking when he had spun his impracticable dream of returning to Cain Springs to Elmer. In lesser degree he had never been free of its urge in his days on the wagon with Isaiah.

He was not unaware that this new world into

which he was stepping included Paula. Somehow it made the prospect even more pleasing, and it so entranced him that he would not have altered a single facet of it had that been possible.

"I guess you're all set," said Roberts.

"I will be as soon as I can get Johnnie's bronc back to him and pick up my work clothes. I'll have to go into the Flat and buy a few things."

"You can't go into town, Kid, until we get back from Lander," Roberts told him. "I want you to be sure about that."

"That's right, David," Ruxton spoke up. "When we get back we're going to pick up Corson at Flat Iron, and the four of us will go in and have a talk with Tuller. We want you to tell your story to Hoke. While we're gone, you stick close to home and keep quiet about Daggett."

The Kid's face fell on learning that he wasn't to accompany the drive. But only for the moment. "You can count on that, Mr. Ruxton. Reckon I'll find plenty to keep me busy. As for talkin' to Hoke Tuller—I don't understand." He glanced questioningly at Grady.

Roberts explained the purpose of the promised conference with the sheriff.

"It's the only way you'll be safe, Kid. It'll pull Daggett's teeth."

"The more it hurts him, the better I'll like it," was the boy's flinty answer. "You figure it'll be all right for me to keep Johnnie's bronc till you get back? He expected me to return it in a day or two."

"I don't see why he couldn't ride over to Double Diamond, Grady," said Ruxton. "Take Paula with you, David. You go tomorrow or the next day. And now you better go in and tell her we've made a deal. She'll be anxious to hear."

11

When Medicine Flat was just a wide place in the road, it had become the practice for stockmen whose ranges lay to the north or east of town to drive through the Flat when they sent their beef cut out to the railroad. Though it had grown and blossomed into the county seat with the passing years, that custom of driving through town still held.

It disrupted business for several hours. The main street had to be cleared of teams and rigs. Furthermore, it wasn't unusual for two or three spooky steers to break away from their fellows and make a wild dash down the plank sidewalk, beneath the wooden awnings of the various business establishments, scattering everything in their path and smashing a window or two. Awning posts were sometimes snapped off, causing the overhanging roof to collapse and leaving the street looking like a tornado had struck it.

But Medicine Flat loved every minute of it; every attempt to forbid the stockmen the use of the street was howled down. To hell with the damage! This was the Flat's chance to show its pride in what it was shipping out to the world!

Owners felt the same way about it. It gave them a chance to show off. As for the crews, they wouldn't have given up this opportunity for a rip-snorting farewell to their friends for anything.

Lee Ruxton enjoyed it more than most owners. He was proud of the white-faced Herefords he raised. Few stockmen in Wyoming had given as much thought as he to improving the blood strains of beef cattle. To send upward of a thousand bawling steers down Medicine Flat's main street, the shrill cries of his men reaching him through the clouds of dust as they hazed the critters along, was always a thrilling experience. Once the great herd had been pressed into the confines of the narrow street, there was something as irresistible about its progress for him as the passing of a conquering army marching through a captured town.

Like a good general, he rode in the rear, his foreman, his trusted lieutenant, at his side. Behind them rumbled the chuck wagon. When from the doorways and second-story windows old friends hailed him, he responded by touching the brim of his hat in a military salute.

This morning—it was barely nine o'clock—two riders dashed into town, yelling: "Quarter Moon drivin' through! Clear the street!"

They rode back and forth, repeating their cry. A scramble at the hitch racks followed as teams and saddle horses were driven into the alleys or openings between the buildings. The Medicine Flat Mercantile Company had a recently arrived assortment of barrels and boxes on the sidewalk in front of the store. Clerks wheeled them inside in a hurry.

Chalk Daggett came out of the sheriff's office and stood on the courthouse steps. He was still in his late thirties, and his muscular, well-knit body was as lean and hard as when he had first come in off the range six years back. His hair and eyes were black as a raven's wing. His face, rocky even in repose, wore an expression even more forbidding than usual this morning.

He had two men with him—Link Hinchman and Frank Ivy. They had been his companions that morning on the Stinking Water. Neither owed him any special allegiance nor bore him any marked good will. He often had Tuller swear them in as special deputies. They picked up a few extra dollars that way. Hinchman owned a livery and feed barn in town. Frank Ivy, when not otherwise engaged, was the Flat's gun- and locksmith. Both men knew of Tuller's promise not to reappoint Daggett and they were not making any secret of the fact that they had an eye on his job.

Chalk's glowering hostility was the result of the news Hinchman had brought him this morning. The latter had just returned from

Double Diamond, where he had gone to pick up a couple of calves for a local butcher. He had found the crew decidedly unfriendly. Words with Ab Byers had brought matters to a head, Ab accusing him of being a party to the killing of Elmer. It was the Kid's story, which Ab had pried out of Johnnie Hines.

Had he not been involved, Hinchman would have welcomed the opportunity to toss Daggett to the wolves. Under the circumstances, however, he had been compelled to make out a case for him, claiming that Chalk had called on Elmer to surrender and had fired only when the cook appeared to be getting away.

Ab had promptly told him he was a liar and made certain other derogatory remarks about Hinchman's forebears, which the latter decided he was in no position to resent at the time, being outnumbered four to one. Hurrying back to the Flat, he had reported his experience to Frank Ivy, who had promptly disclaimed any interest in the matter, since he, unlike Hinchman, had never corroborated Daggett's story of why it had been necessary to kill Big Elmer. Having made that clear, he had accompanied Hinchman around the corner to the sheriff's office and declared himself just as emphatically to Chalk. Their angry three-sided debate had been interrupted by the cry that the Quarter Moon trail herd was coming.

"What's the matter—you afraid to be seen

standin' here with us?" Daggett muttered with an angry rasp as Frank started to move down the steps in the direction of a group of men who had come out of the courthouse.

"That's about the size of it," Ivy retorted. "It might give somebody the wrong impression to see us standin' together."

Daggett flicked him a murderous glance. "You come back to the office afterward! We'll have this out!"

"Keep quiet, Chalk!" Hinchman advised in a heavy whisper. "The Kid's story hasn't got around yet. We can figure out somethin' if we use our heads."

Down the street a shrill cowboy yell announced that the herd was in sight. The cry was taken up and tossed back and forth. Grady had a dozen men in his trail crew. All of them were riding flank.

Presently the first wave of steers charged past the courthouse, tails up and heads lowered. Behind them the street was a sea of glistening backs and flashing horns. In sheer exuberance a man climbed out on the wooden awning in front of the Gem Saloon and emptied a six-gun in the air. There were other shots, more shouting. The frightened cows bellowed lustily. Medicine Flat had seldom been the scene of such bedlam.

The crew kept hazing the herd along, faster and faster, giving it little opportunity to get out of hand. It was the lull before the storm. A little girl was leaning from an upper-story window, waving a flag. The flag slipped out of her hands and came flashing down in a red-and-white spiral. A wild-eyed yearling got a flash of it and bolted out of its path, splintering the drugstore hitch rack and chasing half a dozen men inside the store.

A Quarter Moon rider was on top of the cow as it careened off the front of the building, slapping it across the face with his coiled rope. The panic-stricken critter was not to be turned back by such methods. With a frenzied snort it stampeded up the sidewalk, scattering everything in its path and snapping off an upright in front of the barbershop that left the awning sagging dangerously.

The men gathered at the courthouse beat a quick retreat when the steer started to climb the steps. It lost its footing, however, and went down heavily. Two Quarter Moon punchers were there to haze it back into the street when it scrambled to its feet.

The crowd cheered; no one had been hurt and the damage was negligible.

"That was Rucker and Chick Anson," Hinchman said to Chalk. "That makes seven of 'em."

Daggett nodded. "And here comes Stony Justin."

They were making a careful check of the men Roberts was taking to Lander. Other riders passed, and then came Ruxton and Grady. The latter's roving glance located Daggett. Their eyes locked for a long moment in a hatred that was bitter and implacable.

Daggett shifted his attention to the chuck wagon, expecting to find the Kid on the seat with little Andy Huckins, the long-time Quarter Moon cook. With unexplained satisfaction he saw that Andy was alone.

"They ain't takin' him, Link! They're keepin' the Kid to home!"

"So what?" Hinchman demanded suspiciously. "Don't tell me you're goin' to be damned fool enough to try any rough stuff! You'll go it alone if you do! You get that straight! Things look bad enough right now, and you won't help 'em any by tanglin' with that boy!"

"Suppose you leave that to me," Daggett growled. "Roberts has got a dozen men with him; that means there's only Homer Dorr, Shorty Ryan, and a couple other old-timers on the ranch. I can get to the Kid all right, if that's what I decide to do. I've got a few days to figure out somethin'. Maybe I won't have to get rough with him; maybe I can persuade him to change his story."

"Chalk, you're crazy!" Hinchman whipped out as they pushed into the office. "Roberts knows what happened, and by now I suppose Ruxton and all the rest of 'em have heard it. The kind of persuasion you'll use will be to frame up somethin' on the Kid. If he doesn't agree to clear out of the country in a hurry, you'll muss him up with a gun. I tell you, I won't stand for it!"

"Why don't you shut up?" Daggett rapped contemptuously. He was aware of Frank Ivy standing in the doorway. "What's got into the two of you? I ain't askin' you to do anythin' about the Kid! I can take care of it!"

"Daggett, why don't you take a tumble to yourself?" Ivy demanded coolly. "You're all washed up around here. Why don't you turn in your badge and drift while you got your health?"

"So that's the way it looks to you, eh?" Chalk's mouth curled in a sneer. Rocking with rage, he glared at the two men with slitted eyes. "Get out—the two of you!" he snarled. "And to hell with you! You won't never pick my bones!"

Daggett was left in such a turmoil that the morning was gone before he could settle himself down to planning what his move should be. Old Hoke was home, laid up with one of his recurring attacks of asthma, for which Daggett was thankful. In his present mood he knew he couldn't have stood having the doddering old man about.

All Chalk wanted was a trumped-up charge against the Kid that would hold enough water to frighten the youngster into fleeing the country. Hours of cogitation failed to reward him with an idea that would serve his purpose. When he had gone out with the posse to capture Elmer Lundy he had told the men not to bother about picking up the Kid; that he wasn't interested in bringing a charge against him. He could fully appreciate now what a stupid mistake that had been. It would have been so easy to send out a notice on the boy that would have kept him away from Medicine Flat forever. It was too late now to threaten him with arrest as an accessory in the killing of Trapnell. But Chalk's thoughts continued to dwell on the Kid's flight with Elmer, and he was suddenly electrified to discover what he had been seeking most of the day. The longer he examined it, the more convinced he became that it would do the trick.

"I'll ride out to Quarter Moon tomorrow and see if I can locate him," he promised himself. "He'll play it my way or I'll know why!"

His sinister scheming sent no premonition of impending trouble winging across space to the Kid. Things were going so well with him that no trace of misgiving cast its shadow across his sky. He had moved down to the bunkhouse and got acquainted with old Homer and the other Quarter Moon veterans who had been left behind to run the ranch until the trail crew returned. At first glance he had found himself sharing Paula's enthusiasm for Blue Rocket. She had shown him over the ranch, explaining that the old dirt track was to be harrowed and rolled at once. The railing and fence needed some minor repairs and a coat of whitewash, as did the judges' stand at the finish line. All of this was to be done immediately.

It all partook of the nature of a miracle to the Kid. On the other big ranches where he had worked, if a windowpane got broken or a board needed replacing, nothing was ever done about it. It was different here; if anything needed doing, it got done. Stranger still were the laughter and cheerfulness with which everyone went about his work. The Kid wasn't used to laughter; life had always been a serious business with him.

The arrangement of the box stalls in the barn where Blue Rocket was quartered aroused the Kid's curiosity. Each stall—there were six in all, taking up one side of the barn—could be entered only through an outside door, the upper half of which could be closed or opened independent of the lower half. An overhanging roof, or wooden awning, ran the length of the barn, affording protection against sun and rain.

"Looks to me as though it had been built for a racin' stable," he remarked to Paula.

"It was," she confirmed. "Dad built it the same summer he put in the track. Mother and he planned it together. She was from Kentucky—Fayette County, in the blue grass. That's where I was in school."

The blue grass wasn't beyond the orbit of the Kid's knowledge of the world.

"When I was workin' for Cleve Taylor, his Black John used always to be talkin' about the blue grass and what fast horses they had there. He taught me most of what I know about ridin' a race. I never heard that your father had a big string of thoroughbreds."

Paula shook her head. "He never got around to it, David. Mother passed away that winter, and that was the end of everything for Dad for a long time. He kept Star Gazer for a couple of years and then let him go . . . What made you ask about the stables?"

"I was just thinkin' that it would be a good idea to have one of the stalls cleared out and put Gyp alongside the Rocket." Gyp was the little bronc that Ruxton had put at their disposal. "A horse ain't contented when he's alone; the better they get acquainted, the better they'll work together."

The unused box stalls had become the repository of odds and ends of ranch equipment. The one adjoining the Rocket's stall was piled high with cordwood. The ease with which Paula wheedled old Homer into clearing it out made the Kid grin. "Reckon she'll be tryin' to get around me the same way," he thought.

The job was completed that afternoon, and after the Kid had made the stall ready, Gyp was brought up from the horse corral.

"Glad to be able to do it," Homer declared when Paula thanked him. "But it's a mistake, ma'am, to pamper a bronc. All that fella knows is to go and go. If you and the Kid start pilin' hard grain into him, look out! He'll explode under you one of these mornin's!"

"Don't worry, Homer," the Kid spoke up, "I'll see that Gyp gets enough work to keep him from gettin' spooky."

"All right! I was jest tellin' you. Sure looks nice to see the pair of 'em pokin' their heads out thataway. I'll have Shorty drop a load of hay for you in the mornin'. Is there anythin' else you need?"

"I'll put up some pegs to hang our gear on," the boy answered. "We'll need to string a wire so we can hang up a blanket to dry. I'll take care of all that as soon as I can get into a pair of overalls."

"Yuh!" Homer grunted. He sounded like old Dutch. "Bust a bottle of hoss medicine around here and you'd swear we was back in the racin' game."

"Is that bad?" Paula queried laughingly.

"Shucks, no! I'd walk all the way to Cody to see a good hoss race. You want to keep off the track, Paula, till we git her worked up. I noticed a couple gopher holes at the west turn. I'll poison the dang things outa there tomorrow."

He had a mongrel collie named Fetch. The dog had already attached itself to the Kid. Homer pretended not to be aware of it, for he had often boasted that the collie was a one-man dog and wouldn't pay attention to anyone but him.

"Come on, Fetch!" he called as he started up the yard.

The dog hesitated, glancing at the Kid, and then trotted away in the wake of the old man. After following him a few yards it scampered back to the boy.

"Can't understand it!" Homer grumbled. "That doggone kid seems to be takin' over the whole ranch!"

12

The Kid and Paula were still at the stables when the supper bell rang.

"We better ride over to Double Diamond in the mornin'," she suggested as they were parting in front of the crew's quarters. "You can't do much work in your good clothes." She had a pony named Fluff. She said she'd ride the mare; the Kid could put his saddle on Gyp. "If we get an early start, David, we can be home by noon."

"I'll be waitin' with the horses at the gallery by the time you're done with breakfast," he told her.

Life on Quarter Moon, for all its freedom, was lived according to rule, and they were no less effective because they were not posted in black and white. For one thing, the help didn't go to the house unless on business or by invitation. It was equally true that the family didn't invade the crew's quarters without reason. The Kid didn't have to be told, but his eyes followed Paula hopefully as she hurried across the yard. She didn't look back, and he turned into the bunk-house. It didn't occur to him to ask himself why he would have preferred her company to the salty conversation of such seasoned old-timers as Homer and Shorty Ryan.

In the absence of little Andy, Shorty did the cooking for the men who had been left at home. It fell to the Kid to wash the dishes.

The night was cool enough to make a fire comfortable. The men sat around the stove, talking. The Kid joined them after he had finished in the kitchen. Their chatter held no great interest for him until Shorty began telling of the high times he had had in Chicago back in the days when Quarter Moon used to sell its beef there. That was before cattle buyers began to come West, so that today a stockman could sell his steers on the hoof in almost any railroad town. An experience that was still cameo-clear in Shorty's memory was the night he had seen the Great Wild West Show. He spoke of it familiarly as the Two Bills Show—Buffalo Bill and Pawnee Bill. From the size of the mammoth tent and the grand entrance of the performers, down to the Indian attack on the Deadwood stage, he didn't miss a detail. Best of all, he liked the cowboy band on horseback.

"They had a singer with the band all dressed in white buckskin," he recalled. "Yuh could hear him all over the tent. And sing! Like to tear yore heart out jest listenin' to him! I'd seen plenty Injuns and cow pokes, but that fella in the white buckskin shore took my eye. Paid him a hundred dollars a night, I heard."

"That's pretty steep, Shorty," the Kid put in. "A hundred dollars a night is a heap of money. What was they sellin' with that show?"

Shorty turned on him indignantly. "They wasn't sellin' nuthin'! It wa'n't no medicine show! Yuh had to pay to git in. The cheapest seats was four bits. Talk about a hundred dollars bein' money—why, some of them Eyetalians in the operas git ten times that!"

"Reckon they do," old Homer admitted. "But that kind o' money don't stick with you. Come easy, go easy. When you get old you got nothin'. A man's better off if he just keeps peggin' away and puttin' a few dollars by whenever he can. Look at the boss; that's what he done. And see what he's got today. He can pay a couple thousand dollars for a fast hoss and think no more of it. Ain't nothin' like buildin' up a nice ranch and bein' able to sit back and tell the whole danged world to go to hell."

The Kid lay awake long after he had gone to bed, mulling over what Shorty and Homer had said. No doubt but that Homer had it right; there couldn't be anything nicer than owning a big spread like Quarter Moon. But a hundred dollars a night just for singing. The Kid couldn't get over it. "He must have been an awful good singer," he concluded with a faint pang of envy.

• • •

Paula and he got away early, cutting across Quarter Moon range for a long mile and then following the county road to Double Diamond. They were just in time to catch Johnnie.

"I'd have passed yuh on the road if yuh hadn't got here when yuh did," he told the Kid. "I've got to go into the Flat for the old man."

He knew Paula by sight. He called her Miss Ruxton.

"I wanted to get your bronc back to you," the Kid said. "And I need the clothes I left with you. I'm workin' for Quarter Moon."

"I figgered yuh must be. If yuh'll wait up a minute, Miss Ruxton, I'll turn the pony into the corral and ride back a piece with you. Yuh can come down to the corral with me, Kid. Yore bundle is still in the wagon. We'll stop at the barn and yuh can pick it up."

Johnnie had something on his mind, and he got to it as soon as they were alone. It concerned the altercation between Ab and Hinchman.

"I wasn't around, Kid, or I'd have stopped Ab from shootin' off his mouth."

The Kid stared at him accusingly. "How did you come to tell Ab?"

"I dunno! I didn't mean to tell him. But hell, Kid, Chalk was dead shore to find out yuh was back and—"

"He's found out all right, Johnnie! And he

knows what I saw!" The Kid was angry through and through and not trying to hide the fact. "It's a fine note—comin' with Grady and Mr. Ruxton gone to Lander with the drive! I give 'em my word I wouldn't let nothin' slip till they got back!"

"I don't blame yuh for bein' sore," said Johnnie. "It was Ab's fault—"

"It was your fault! You did the blabbin'! Grady was afraid Daggett might try to do somethin' to me . . . You give me my gun. I ain't takin' no chances with him."

Johnnie nodded. "I better let yuh have it. But don't go lookin' for trouble, y'understand?"

Neither of them said anything to Paula about the incident as they jogged along, but she surmised that something was wrong.

"Yuh ain't got much of a piece to go now!" Johnnie called out to them as they turned off the road for home. "Better stick close to the house, Kid, till Grady gits back!"

Paula demanded an explanation as soon as she and the boy were alone. The Kid was frank with her.

"Too bad the damn fool couldn't keep his mouth shut!" she snapped. "You might have known he'd spill the beans!"

They had loped along for half a mile when Paula saw the Kid rein in sharply.

"What is it?" she demanded anxiously.

"That clump of buckbrush where we come out of this draw! Don't you see that piebald bronc standin' there?"

"Yes, I do!" Paula got out, her throat tight. "That's the horse Chalk Daggett rides!"

"It's Daggett," the Kid said tensely. "He's got us cut off. You turn around, Paula, and catch Johnnie. Get him back here as quick as you can. He can't be more than passin' the Flat Iron house."

"David, I'm afraid to leave you alone with him!"

"I ain't runnin' from him!" The Kid's tone was cold and adamant. "He knows we saw him; he's comin' this way. Get goin', Paula!"

In this emergency his was the voice of authority. She wheeled Fluff and pulled the mare to a driving gallop. The Kid didn't take his eyes off Daggett.

"That's close enough!" he called out when Chalk was within fifty paces of him. "I can hear anythin' you got to say from there!"

His hand was inside the bundle of clothes on his saddle horn, clutching the gun. Finding himself face to face with Chalk whipped up the last drop of hatred he bore the man. It took him back to that morning on the Stinking Water. He could see Elmer tumbling out of his saddle again.

Daggett pulled his horse to a stop. "Kid, you're goin' on the prod before you're hurt," he announced, trying to put a counterfeit friendliness in his voice. He surmised that Paula had left to bring up reinforcements. "I just heard that you was around again. I got a little matter to talk over with you."

"Get to the point, Daggett!" the Kid whipped out fiercely. "What do you want with me?"

"Kid—when you pulled away from Flat Iron's line camp the night Joe Trapnell was killed, you helped yourself to a horse. I'm not interested in whether you sold it, traded it off, or turned it adrift. All I know is that it was never returned to Corson."

The Kid stiffened. He got the threat Daggett was conveying. "Corson owed me my winter's wages; that took care of the bronc."

"How much did you have comin'?"

"Twenty-seven dollars."

"No, Kid, that won't do," Chalk said flatly. "You know better'n to tell me you can buy a good bronc for that money. But we're wastin' time; your bookkeepin' doesn't mean anythin' to me. Accordin' to the law, you stole that horse. You know what that means."

The Kid was scared, but not to the point of losing his wits. "Is Corson chargin' me with stealin' the horse?"

"Not yet. I don't suppose he knows you're back. It's my duty to tell him. Just as soon as he signs a warrant it'll be up to me to take you in.

If you're smart you'll go along with me now."

"Not a chance, Daggett!" was the Kid's emphatic answer. "I ain't givin' myself up on your say-so!"

Chalk had made the suggestion in the confident belief that it would be rejected. Nevertheless, he was relieved to have this judgment confirmed; arresting the boy was the last thing in the world he intended doing. All he hoped to gain by the subterfuge was to put a little more pressure on him.

"Okay!" Chalk muttered, picking up his reins as though ready to let it go at that. He knew Paula Ruxton would have to go no farther than the Flat Iron house to enlist aid. He didn't propose to be caught here and have to face Corson.

"Just a minute!" the Kid exclaimed. He was getting his nerve back. "Why didn't you get your warrant before you looked me up, Daggett?"

It was a question Chalk had hoped to avoid.

"I can tell you!" the Kid growled. "You wanted to give me a chance to high-tail it out of Wyomin' again! I know too much, Daggett! You don't want me around—in jail or out of it!"

"To hell with what you know!" Chalk snarled. He wasn't fooling now; out of the corner of his eye he had seen half a dozen riders turn off the road, running their ponies hard. "I'm givin' you twenty-four hours to come to your senses! I don't know who this bunch is the girl's got with her, but you keep your mouth shut or you'll get knocked off!"

Paula had overtaken Johnnie just beyond the Flat Iron house. In the ranch yard they found Reb Corson, old Dutch, and two other riders. What Johnnie had to say supplied all the explanation they needed.

"You stay behind, Paula!" Reb yelled as they flashed out of the yard. He could just as well have saved his breath; using the quirt on Fluff, she raced out ahead of the others and held her position until they swept down into the draw. She hadn't been sure what she expected to find, but seeing the Kid sitting there on Gyp, apparently unharmed, snapped the tension in her and she suddenly felt faint.

"What goes on here?" Corson demanded of Chalk.

Pretending to ignore the hostile faces ringed about him, Daggett jerked his head in the Kid's direction. "Do you recognize him, Reb?"

"Naturally! But that ain't answering me! What's your business with him?"

"The usual business of the sheriff's office. It shouldn't be necessary for me to tell you the law's got a grudge against the Kid. I don't know what call you got to get excited when we're lookin' out for your interests. At the inquest into the killin' of Joe Trapnell you testified the Kid had stole one of your horses."

"Hell, I didn't say nothin' of the sort!" Corson returned. "I said the Kid had run off with one of my broncs."

Daggett shrugged patronizingly. "Run off, Reb? That's only another way of sayin' the same thing. The law calls it by a harder name. You've never reported gettin' the horse back."

"That's right, I never did say anything further about it," Corson admitted, some of the belligerence fading from his voice. "I've got to blame myself for that; but never having made a formal complaint, I didn't figure it was up to me to let you or Hoke know the matter had been settled to my satisfaction."

"What do you mean—settled?" Chalk inquired with marked uneasiness. For a moment he had thought he was making his point.

"I owed the Kid some money—about half the value of the animal. Roberts came to me and made good the difference." Reb swung his horse around and focused his attention on the boy. "Is that all Daggett was putting up to you, Kid?"

"That's about the size of it, Reb," was the Kid's studied answer. "He warned me he'd be out tomorrow to pick me up if you signed the warrant."

"Warnin' yuh, my foot!" Johnnie whipped out in hot indignation. "He was tryin' to scare the daylights out of yuh so yuh'd make yourself scarce!" His eyes drilled into Chalk. "Yuh ain't puttin' nothin' over on me, Daggett! When yuh want a party, yuh show up with the papers—yuh don't tip him off that yo're goin' to be wantin' him!"

Johnnie looked around at Dutch and the others. The Kid's failure to accuse Daggett appeared to have them confused, and they were satisfied to leave it to Corson to do their talking.

"Seems to me this is a case of much ado about nothing," said Reb. "If there's any more talk about a horse-stealing charge being brought against you, Kid, pay no attention to it. I accepted payment for the bronc, and that settles it . . . Do you understand it that way, Daggett?"

"I don't see how I could understand it any other way," Chalk growled. "Too bad I didn't know before; I could have saved myself some trouble!"

It was a gross understatement, and he was fully aware of it; his scheme had not only failed but had backfired so badly that it was idle to think now that any trick could be devised that would frighten the Kid into making a quick disappearance.

Daggett's respect for the boy had grown tremendously in the past few minutes. Instead of taking up Johnnie's blistering attack and adding a blast of his own, the Kid had held his tongue, and not because he was afraid to speak, Daggett was sure. The Kid was playing a game—holding back for a reason. For the moment it gave him the upper hand. It led Chalk to conclude that the boy might get him out of this situation, and though he didn't know where it was leading him, he decided to risk it.

"Appears as though there's been a misunderstandin' all around," he said. "It wasn't necessary for Miss Ruxton to rush away to get you and your boys, Reb. I couldn't have taken the Kid into custody without his consent. I told him the smart thing for him to do was to come along with me. If he had, I'd have stopped at Flat Iron. When I heard your side of it I'd have had to let him go, and that would have been the end of it."

Corson continued to regard him with narrowed eyes, his leathery face expressionless. "I don't hear you saying anything about the boy's story of what he saw on the Stinking Water the morning Big Elmer Lundy was killed. Wasn't that what you really had on your mind in laying out here for him? Reckon you know what I'm referring to."

Chalk nodded. "I heard it yesterday. It doesn't bother me; I've got a couple witnesses who saw it different. I didn't even mention it to the Kid."

Reb whirled around on the boy. "Is that right?"

"Neither one of us said anythin' about it, Reb," the Kid told him. "If he was goin' to say anythin' he hadn't got to it. All his talk was about the horse I took."

Johnnie was violently disappointed. "We got

here too quick, I reckon! There'd have been another story to tell if we hadn't showed up! . . . Reb, you see Daggett to the road; I'll ride a piece with the Kid and Miss Ruxton."

Grumbling to himself, he jogged off with Paula and David.

"That was awful white of Grady—squarin' me with Reb," the Kid observed, not speaking to either in particular. "I got the money to make it good when he gets home. I sure thought Daggett had me over a barrel."

"Yeh!" was Johnnie's monosyllabic comment.

Paula rode on without saying anything, her green eyes flashing with annoyance. Finally she could hold in no longer. "You didn't have to make a fool of me, David! If you were going to agree with everything he said, why did you send me off for help? Were you afraid to talk?"

"Yeh!" Johnnie chimed in. "That's what I want to know, Kid! Yuh could have said more'n yuh did. Daggett was puttin' the squeeze on yuh, wasn't he?"

The Kid nodded grimly. "He didn't run into me by accident."

"I knew it! Why did yuh hold back?"

"I reckoned it would keep till Grady got home. It may take Daggett a day or two to figure that out, but he'll get around to it!"

13

When Paula came down to the stables that afternoon she had gotten over her annoyance with the Kid. She could see he had been busy, and she complimented him on the way he had things looking.

"How's the Rocket, David?"

"Fine! He's gettin' used to me. I curried him and he didn't twitch a muscle. He and Gyp seem to be hittin' it off all right. I see Homer's gettin' busy on the track."

"It'll take them two or three days," said Paula. "I suppose after we get on it it'll be slow; the ground's so dry it won't pack. We need a good rain."

The Kid saddled the horses.

"You take the Rocket and I'll get up on Gyp," Paula told him. "You'll find he's got a rather tough mouth for a two-year-old, David. You don't have to be afraid of hurting him."

They jogged the horses up and down the yard until they were warm. Afterward they took them on the dirt road that ran into Medicine Flat for an hour.

"That's enough!" the Kid called out. "He's really hot!"

"How does he handle?" Paula asked as they jogged home.

"Fine! He likes to run. You can't tell much about him yet, but he puts his feet down like he was runnin' on velvet."

They saw no more of Daggett. The Kid had the afternoons to himself, and he took to riding off on Gyp, with Fetch running along with him, to explore Quarter Moon range.

Paula knew he had the gun, and it troubled her.

"I wish you'd give it to Homer for safekeeping until Grady gets home," she told him one morning.

The Kid shook his head. Not wanting to be questioned, he had said nothing to Homer and the other men about his encounter with Chalk.

"After what happened the other day, I'm packin' it along when I go out in the afternoon," he declared emphatically. "I might need it."

Paula stared at him, aghast. "Do you mean to tell me you'd use a gun on him?"

"I would if I had to," the Kid answered doggedly.

"It would be the stupidest thing you could do!" she protested. "It would only be giving him an excuse to do something terrible to you! If you won't give it up now, you will as soon as Father gets back! I'll see to that!"

Paula left the argument standing there and went up to the house.

"Layin' the law down to me already!" the Kid complained to himself. "You'd think I was some tenderfoot!"

Little Medicine Creek came down from the high places through the Slash Hills to form the western boundary of Quarter Moon. In its lower course it crossed the road from the ranch to town. West of the creek the Slash Hills were a tangled mass of badlands of so little value to stockmen that they were still in the public domain.

Quarter Moon cattle had beaten down numerous trails to the creek. To keep his stock from drifting across it, Ruxton had strung a five-strand fence along it for several miles. Old Homer mentioned the creek to the Kid at noon.

"If yo're jest goin' out for the ride, Kid, why don't you put a fishline in yore pocket and bring us back a mess of rainbows? The water's cold enough to make 'em fine eatin'."

The suggestion interested the Kid.

"There's some big holes jest above the old cabin," Homer explained. "You can't miss it if you'll jest follow our fence. You can cut yoreself a pole and crawl through the wire most anyplace. I'll tie up Fetch so he won't tag along and spoil the fishin'."

He supplied hook and line and helped to dig a canful of worms.

Forty minutes of easy riding put the Kid on the creek. The clouds that had been piling up in the west all morning had finally blanketed the sun, and there was every reason to believe that rain, which Paula had said they needed, would fall before evening.

The gray afternoon didn't disturb the Kid. He liked wild country, and under a leaden sky the Slash Hills had a brooding somberness that gave him a thrilling sense of isolation and adventure.

Instead of descending to the creek bottoms, the Kid followed the bluffs above the brawling stream. It wasn't long before he picked up the Quarter Moon fence and, in another mile, caught his first glimpse of the tumble-down cabin Homer had described. Windows and doors were gone. Though its shake roof was still intact, it was beginning to sag badly.

According to Homer, the cabin was there, looking about the same as it did today when he first went to work for Ruxton, now a matter of over thirty years ago. He didn't know who had built it but supposed that some trapper had made it his headquarters. Quarter Moon riders, caught out in a storm, often sought its shelter, he said.

The Kid could see a patch of barren, hard-packed ground in front of the door where horses had been tethered. A white cedar had taken root in the doorway and was now five feet high. Scrub brush was marching in close to the cabin in every direction. It wasn't like Cain Springs, sun-baked and barren, but it was equally forlorn, and the Kid was conscious of it.

"I'll have a closer look at it on my way back," he thought. "I may have to duck in there to get out of this rain squall."

When he located the trout holes Homer had mentioned he found it impossible to find a way down with a horse. A surprise awaited him when he swung out of the saddle: padding along the trail behind him was as big a coyote as he had ever seen.

The startled animal froze in its tracks for a moment, giving the Kid time enough to draw his gun and fire. The bark of the shot released the coyote from its trance and it bounded away unharmed.

"What a gun!" the Kid burst out scornfully. "I like to broke my finger pullin' the trigger! You couldn't hit the side of a barn with it!"

He tethered the pony and was about to crawl down the steep bank to the creek, when he heard a commotion on the trail. A moment later Fetch scampered into view. The gnawed piece of rope trailing from his collar told what had happened.

"So you found me, did you!" the Kid exclaimed, giving the dog a hug. "Homer was afraid you'd spoil my fishin', so you keep behind me, hear?"

When he reached the creek the Kid took a look at the water before cutting himself a willow pole and found it so roiled that there was no chance of his catching a few trout.

"Been stormin' hard up above," he said to Fetch. "A trout couldn't see a worm."

He tossed in a handful and saw them float away without a fish rising to grab them. No further proof was needed that fishing that afternoon would be a waste of time. He took it philosophically and sat down on a dry boulder and smoked a cigarette. Fetch crawled up to him on his belly and begged a little attention.

"You're quite a customer, mister," the Kid declared, stroking the dog's ears affectionately. "I never owned a dog. When I was movin' around so much I couldn't look out for one. But I'm settled down now. I sure wish Homer'd give you to me."

Fetch licked his hand and wagged his tail as though to say he understood and approved.

The minutes fled as they tarried at the edge of the pool. A few drops of rain fell and aroused the Kid from his dreamy meditation.

"Maybe we better get out of here, Fetch," he observed, studying the patch of sky visible between the tops of the overhanging cedars. "I bet the thunder really rolls some in these hills when she gets goin' good."

He scrambled up the bank to the pony. The rain held off, however, and he took his time about mounting. When he finally swung up and started back along the trail, Fetch brought up the rear, having been trained to follow a horse and never to lead it.

The Kid sighted the old cabin before long. He had spent so much time up above that he decided he would look it over another time, though the rain was beginning to come down in earnest.

"Must be gettin' on to five o'clock," he mused aloud. "I'll take a wettin' rather than get in late."

Thinking of it later and trying to recall what had made him pull up sharply and order Fetch to be quiet, he was at a loss to decide whether it had been the snapping of brush or a movement in the trees on the far side of the creek, caught subconsciously out of the corner of his eye, that had warned him that someone was approaching the cabin. Alert, nerves tense, he sat there watching, safely screened by the trees. In a moment or two he caught sight of Daggett's familiar piebald bronc.

Chalk was pushing the animal hard and without regard for the tough going.

The Kid's first thought was that Daggett was looking for him. To his surprise, Chalk pulled up in front of the cabin, dropped the reins over his pony's head, and darted inside.

"It can't be the rain," the Kid thought. "It ain't comin' down that hard yet."

He pulled back from the trail a few feet and slid to the ground. Squatting down on his toes, he put an arm around Fetch and cautioned the dog again to be quiet. He was two hundred feet or more above the creek. With the steep bank and the fence standing between them, he was sure he could get away without being overtaken, even if Daggett saw him. He had no thought of leaving. Indeed, wild horses couldn't have pulled him away. There was something mysterious and unexplainable about Chalk's business at the cabin, and the Kid's white-lipped curiosity had him chained to the spot.

Not more than ten minutes had passed when he saw Daggett brush past the scrub cedar that had sprung up in the doorway and hurry to his horse. He glanced about suspiciously, and then, apparently convinced that he was unobserved, mounted and struck west into the hills.

Though the Kid shook off the tautness that had gripped him, Daggett's visit to the cabin became more mysterious than ever.

"By grab, I'm goin' down there and try to find out what he was up to!" he muttered. "He didn't come up here for nothin'!"

For the second time that afternoon he crawled down the bank and went through the wire, with Fetch at his heels.

The cabin was a one-room affair. Through the years cowpunchers had ripped up the plank flooring for firewood, so that nothing remained but the four walls and the roof.

The Kid looked it over carefully. Thinking Daggett might have left a note for someone, he examined the chinks in the logs but found nothing. His bewilderment grew. The place had a dank, moldy smell. He sniffed the air but could detect nothing more than the heavy odor of rotting wood.

"Stumps me!" he declared. "If there's anythin' queer here, I can't see it!" Fetch was digging busily in the corner. "Come on, Fetch! You let that mouse go; we'll be gettin' along home."

The dog voiced an excited "Woof! Woof!" and continued its digging.

"Come on, I tell you," the Kid repeated sharply.

He heard the dog's claws grating on metal.

"What you got there, Fetch?" he asked, only mildly interested.

He pushed the dog aside and saw a rusted tin can lying in the hole. He bent over and pulled it out.

"Jee-rusalem!" he gasped as he glimpsed its contents. It was stuffed with paper money, so tightly jammed into the can that he had difficulty extracting the roll. Bug-eyed, he stared at the bills. "So that was it! This is what Daggett was hidin' here!"

He was too excited to count the money carefully, but he saw there was better than fifteen thousand dollars in the roll.

Was this Daggett's nest egg? Was he getting

ready to pull out of the country on the double-quick?

It left the Kid groping for the right answer. He had never imagined Chalk's job had been that profitable.

He laughed suddenly, a harsh, bitter laugh that held all the hatred he bore Chalk Daggett. He had him where he wanted him now. When Chalk came looking for his money it wouldn't be here! He could look his eyes out and he wouldn't find it!

"This will help square Elmer's account!" the boy growled as he filled up the hole and tamped down the damp earth. He could feel the roll of bills heavy in his pocket. It drove him on as though he were possessed.

When the cache showed no sign of having been disturbed, the Kid hurried out. Pausing only to pick up a can from the many strewn about, he climbed the bank and rode away quickly. Half a mile from the cabin he put the money in the can and hid it beneath the exposed roots of a dead cedar.

For the first time it occurred to him that the money was now his, if he wanted it that way; that he could let it lie there for as long as he pleased, then dig it up. It wouldn't be as though he had stolen it—not quite.

The Kid struggled with that moral problem for a minute and then decided to put it behind him for the present. He wouldn't say anything to anyone—not even to Grady. Not for the present, at least.

Riding homeward through the rain, he mastered his excitement; he knew he had to act as though nothing had happened. Otherwise one question would lead to another and he'd betray his secret.

On riding into the yard he promptly had his own problems whisked out of his head. Ruxton's yellow-wheeled buckboard stood at the gallery steps, with Homer holding the horses. A dozen broncs stood at the hitch rack in front of the bunkhouse. It could only mean that the trail crew was back. They hadn't been expected for another day. But here they were, and there was Grady, clad in a slicker, coming across the yard from his cottage.

The Kid couldn't have explained the sudden feeling of anxiety that whipped through him. An air of tenseness seemed to have descended on the ranch, as though tragedy had struck it. He didn't see Paula come out of the house dressed for town, but she ran down the steps, calling to him.

"David, where have you been this afternoon?" she demanded breathlessly.

"Why—I just been up above a ways," he answered with conscious vagueness.

"You went up the creek, didn't you?" The Kid

was about to avoid a direct answer, when Paula said, "You don't have to say! Homer told me you had gone fishing."

"I changed my mind; I didn't do any fishin'."

Was it possible, he asked himself, that she knew about the money he had found?

Paula drew herself up, her young face grave and distraught. "David—let me see your gun!"

The Kid handed it over, too puzzled by her questions and manner to know what impended.

Paula broke it expertly and put her nose to the barrel. "It's been fired—hasn't it?"

"I tried to kill a coyote," the Kid explained, stung by the accusing note in her voice.

Grady had come up to them. Paula buried her face against him. "Grady, he couldn't have done it!" she sobbed. "But what am I to think? He was on the creek—and look at this gun! He says he shot at a coyote—"

"If that's what he says, you can believe him," Roberts assured her without hesitation. "The Kid's as innocent of this as you are, Paula . . . What about the gun, Kid? Where did you get it?"

The boy's explanation satisfied the tall man. He called Homer and told him to take charge of the pistol.

Their talk was a ghastly riddle to the Kid. What Paula had said left no doubt but that he was suspected of something, but he knew there couldn't be any connection between the gun and the money he had removed from its hiding place in the cabin.

"Will somebody tell me what it is I'm supposed to have done?" he demanded fearfully.

"You're not supposed to have done anything," Roberts told him. "It's just a coincidence you were on the creek this afternoon and had that gun on you. It was on your account that we speeded things up and clipped off a day. I didn't think we were coming back to run into this . . . Kid, Mr. Ruxton was shot and robbed on his way out from town. Somebody was waiting for him at the ford."

"No!" David gasped, his eyes torn wide with horror. "I'm beginnin' to understand a lot of things! . . . Paula, I'd rather be dead than have you think I had anythin' to do with it. I didn't know your dad was showin' up today."

"Course you didn't, David," she acknowledged, clutching his hand. "I believe you. You know I do! I've just gone to pieces so completely I don't know what I'm doing."

"You've got to pull yourself together, Paula," said Roberts. "I told you your father isn't badly wounded. Whoever held him up has had so much time to get away that it wouldn't do any good to turn the crew out to scour the country. After I took your father to Doc Gentry's office I saw Tuller. Asthma or no asthma, he said he'd go out right away. I'll be surprised, though, if he accomplishes anything."

"If Dad's all right I don't care about the money," said Paula, dabbing at her eyes. "That's all that matters!"

The Kid longed to tell her who had shot her father; that the money was safe. Fear closed his lips. How could he prove his innocence if he took them to the tree where he had hidden the can? Why should they believe his story that he had seen Daggett at the old cabin and all the rest of it? No, he'd have to return the money to the hole where Fetch had found it before he could speak.

"Doesn't anybody know how it happened?" he asked.

"Not much," Grady replied. He put a slicker over Paula's shoulders and helped her into the rig. "I left the Flat ahead of the boss. I wasn't so far ahead of him but that I heard the shot. I raced back and found him lying on the ground. I couldn't see anyone, but I thought I heard the brush cracking to the north of the road. I fired a couple shots at random. I'm taking Paula into town, Kid. If you want to go along, hop on the back seat. There's a slicker on the floor you can use."

The Kid slipped down from the saddle. Giving Gyp a slap on the withers that sent him loping down the yard, he climbed into the buckboard.

Grady got the team moving at once. The Kid

rode with his head lowered against the beating rain and had nothing further to say. But his thoughts were beating a tattoo in his brain. It was becoming increasingly clear to him that, while returning the money to its original place would free him of suspicion, it would not prove Daggett's guilt. The cabin would have to be watched night and day until he came to dig up his loot, so that he could be caught with the money in his possession.

The Kid thought it out carefully. "That's the only way to handle it," he said to himself. "I got a little time; Daggett won't go near the cabin till things quiet down."

14

Night had fallen by the time they reached the doctor's house. Gentry was a bachelor. He kept the rooms on the lower floor for emergency cases such as this and had a practical nurse on call. It was the nearest thing to a hospital that Medicine Flat provided.

Paula and Roberts hurried inside, leaving the Kid to take care of the team.

Gentry's news was good: Ruxton had recovered consciousness and was resting easily. "It's a bad scalp wound and nothing more," he told them. "I've got him in bed. I'll keep him here tonight, but I'll let you take him home tomorrow."

He showed them in.

The Kid drove around in back and put the team in the shed, after which he took a seat in the waiting room. He could hear Grady and Paula talking and gathered at once that Ruxton was out of danger.

Tom McPartland, the district attorney, came in a short while later and asked the nurse to call the doctor out. Not only the amount of money stolen but Ruxton's prominence in the community made it the most important crime McPartland had had to deal with in his many years in office. He wanted to know if Ruxton's condition would permit the asking of some questions. Gentry said yes.

"That's fine," McPartland declared. "I've left word for Tuller to come over as soon as he gets in. He ought to be along in a few minutes."

When old Hoke arrived he had Daggett with him. The latter ignored the Kid and filed into the bedroom with McPartland and Hoke.

The questioning quickly developed an angle that had the boy sitting on the edge of his chair.

"There's no question but that robbery was the sole motive, Lee," the district attorney proclaimed. "It wasn't a case of someone being out to get you. Whoever held you up knew you had a sum of money on you and very likely knew it was your beef money—fifteen to twenty thousand dollars."

"I don't get your point, Tom," said Ruxton. "I thought that was obvious."

"Not at all! It's true, isn't it, that established stock buyers like Henry Brothers and Courtland often pay by check?"

"Yes—"

"Who knew you were paid in currency this time?"

Ruxton thought a moment. "Roberts knew, and I suppose the crew did. I suppose half a dozen people in Lander knew it too."

"That's what I was driving at," McPartland declared. "It had to be someone who knew you got currency. I want you to tell me exactly what you did when you got back to the Flat."

"I didn't do anything unusual. It was too late to get into the bank. I didn't tell anybody I had the money on me. Grady said he was sending the crew on home and that as soon as he got his hair cut he'd go out, too, unless I wanted him to wait for me. It never occurred to me that I might be stuck up or I'd have asked him to wait. I owed the Mercantile Company a bill for groceries and other things—about three hundred dollars—and I dropped in and paid it."

"Was there anyone else in the store at the time?"

"I think there was, but they were up in front. I walked back to the office. Coulter was there alone. I just paid the bill; I didn't say anything to him about the money I was packing around. We talked things over for a few minutes. John wanted to know about the horse I brought up from California. It was raining when I came out. I walked around to the post office and got the mail and read it. I said hello to Ed Hughes. That was all. I got in the saddle and started home."

"Not much of a lead in that," said McPartland. "God knows John Coulter didn't dash out to the ford to rob you. Just the same, I'd like to ask

John a question or two. Hoke, have Daggett go down to the store and ask Coulter to come up here, right away if he can."

Daggett hurried out. The Kid eyed him contemptuously. "You won't be swellin' around much longer!" he promised himself. "I'll put you away where you belong!"

"I'm not overlooking the possibility that someone followed you up from Lander, Lee, and waylaid you," McPartland remarked. "I know it's an outside chance."

He asked Roberts to tell him what he knew about the case. Grady had nothing to add to what he had told Paula and the Kid.

"What about the crew?" the district attorney inquired. "Did they arrive at the ranch together?"

"They did. Huckins drove in with the wagon right behind them."

"That rules them out," McPartland admitted. "You say you heard a shot and turned back at once. There's nothing so unusual about hearing a shot in this country. What gave you the idea Ruxton was in trouble?"

"I knew he was following me out from town and that he had a large sum of money on him . . . Why don't you put your cards on the table, McPartland, and say what you're thinking?" Grady's voice remained low, but its tone was flat and challenging. "Maybe I didn't turn back. Maybe I was waiting at the ford for the boss to come along. Maybe I did this job."

"Grady, no!" Ruxton exclaimed. "Don't even suggest it! I'm sure Tom isn't thinking anything of the sort."

"I'm just trying to test what little evidence there is," said McPartland.

"Mebbe I can shed a little light on it," Hoke spoke up. "Chalk and I went over the ground at the crossin' inch by inch. You know how the brush grows thick close to the north edge of the ford. Back in the willows we found fresh hoss droppin's and enough tracks to leave no doubt about where this gent had waited for Lee . . .. What's the caliber of your gun, Grady?"

"It's a Forty-five."

"That checks," said Hoke.

"What do you mean by that?" came from McPartland.

From a vest pocket Hoke produced an empty .44-caliber cartridge. "I picked this up among the willows. It hadn't lain there long, you can see." From another pocket came two empty .45-caliber shells. "I found these on the bank at the crossin'. It tallies all the way around with Roberts's story. What he says about this unknown party headin' north after the robbery is true, too; the rain's makin' a mess of the tracks, but Chalk and I followed them two to three hundred yards until they hit hard ground."

"Well, that's something definite at last!" the

prosecutor exclaimed. "It gives you a clean bill of health, Grady."

Paula laughed sarcastically. "You're a wonderful detective, Mr. McPartland! Telling us Grady didn't do it! I hope you're convinced that Daddy didn't shoot himself."

"Paula!" her father cried in sharp reprimand.

McPartland took it good-naturedly. "She's right, Lee. Trying to get anywhere on just circumstantial evidence can make a better lawyer than I am look foolish."

Paula came out and sat down with the Kid. Her green eyes were snapping. "Did you ever hear anything so stupid, David?"

"I dunno about that," he replied soberly. "It ain't no worse'n you tryin' to blame it on me. I could put a bug in McPartland's ear!"

Paula straightened up and gave him a searching glance. "David! You know who did it?"

The Kid withdrew into his shell immediately. "I ain't sayin' nothin' till I can prove it. Here comes Daggett and John Coulter."

Coulter was the pivot around which the business life of the community revolved. His sympathy for Ruxton was far outweighed by his indignation over the murderous attack. "Tom, I don't care if it means turning this country upside down, you and Hoke have got to get to the bottom of this," he told McPartland. "Things have reached a sorry state when one of our leading stockmen can be struck down and robbed in broad daylight."

"We're doing everything we can, John," the district attorney assured him. "That's why I asked you to come down. When Lee was in the store this afternoon paying his bill, he says there was just the two of you back at the office. Is that correct?"

"Yes, just the two of us."

"I suppose you gathered, when he paid you in cash, that he had come back from Lander with his steer money in currency."

"He didn't say anything, but I took it for granted," Coulter acknowledged. "I certainly didn't say anything to anyone about it. After he went out I walked up in front and waited on a customer; Mrs. Watts, it was."

"And you had no conversation with anyone about Lee having been in?"

"I wouldn't say that. Chalk came in. He said something about Quarter Moon being back from Lander. I said I knew it; that Lee had just been in to square up his account. That was all. I waited on a couple people and then went back to the warehouse to check a shipment of hardware that had come in that afternoon. I was home having supper when I heard the news."

"That's all I wanted to know from you, John," said McPartland. "It doesn't help me much, but thanks just the same. I'm trying to discover just who knew Lee had a big sum of money in his pocket."

Coulter talked for a few minutes about an organized search for the gunman. No one present seemed to find the suggestion worth while.

"Gentlemen, I think you better let Lee get some rest," Dr. Gentry advised. "I don't want him to overtax himself."

"I guess you're right, Doc," McPartland agreed. "We'll break this up."

"Just a minute, Mac," said Roberts. "Are you still testing what little evidence you have, as you told me?"

The district attorney's head came up sharply. "I certainly am," he said.

"Then why not examine Mr. Coulter's remarks a little more carefully? When he told Daggett that Mr. Ruxton had been in to pay a bill, wasn't that just the same as telling him the boss had his steer money on his person?"

"I been waitin' for somethin' like that from you!" Chalk exclaimed resentfully. "I'd expect you to try to pin this, or anythin' else that happened, on me!"

"I'm not pinning anything on you," Grady returned coolly. "I'm not saying you had anything to do with the robbery, but when Mr. Coulter told you the boss had paid his bill, you could guess the rest. If Mr. Ruxton had come back from Lander with a check for his cattle he wouldn't have been around paying bills."

The Kid had jerked erect, as poised and alert as a bird dog on a fresh scent. He knew Grady had put his finger on the only way in which Daggett could have been tipped off.

"By Joseph, you're right, Roberts!" Coulter declared. "I let the cat out of the bag without knowing it. Now wait a minute, Chalk!" he cautioned as Daggett leaped to his feet to protest his innocence. "As Roberts says, nobody's accusing you of anything, but if you thought about it at all, you must have realized Ruxton had come back with a pocketful of cash."

"And I suppose I knew that he didn't intend to catch up with Roberts and the two of them ride home together!" Daggett whipped out derisively. "I was around town all afternoon. I'll be glad to answer any questions the district attorney wants to ask me."

"Calm down, Chalk," McPartland told him. "We're not going to solve this riddle tonight. But something will turn up that'll give us a lead . . . Hoke, I want the two of you to drop into the saloons tonight and see if you can pick up anything. If you do, get in touch with me first thing in the morning."

When they left, Grady called Paula in to say good night to her father.

"Daddy, I don't want to leave you here alone," Paula protested.

Ruxton put his arm around her. "You run along with Grady. This thing was something of a shock; I'll be better for staying here tonight. You can come in for me tomorrow afternoon. I brought a little something back for you from Lander. It's in my saddlebag. Grady can get it for you."

Paula shook her head. "I'd rather wait and have you give it to me yourself."

"All right, honey," Ruxton told her, pleased that she wanted it that way. "How are you and David doing with the Rocket?"

"We've had him on the road every day. Homer has been working on the track. This rain will help things." She refrained from saying anything about the meeting with Chalk. "David came in with us. He's out in the waiting room."

"Well, send him in, Paula! I'd like to see him."

The Kid heard, and he was embarrassed and wanted to run.

"You shouldn't have told him I was here," he whispered to Paula. "I ain't in no shape to go in there in these old duds—my boots covered with mud."

"Don't be silly," she replied, taking him by the arm.

Ruxton had a friendly greeting for the boy. The Kid stood beside the bed, fingering his hat nervously.

"I don't like to see you with your head tied up that way, Mr. Ruxton," he managed to say. "I—I wouldn't worry about the money. You'll get it back."

Ruxton smiled ruefully. "I wish I were half as confident as you are about it. But whether I get it back or not, we'll make out. You better take these youngsters into Charlie's restaurant and get them supper, Grady. I'll see you tomorrow."

"I'll let you out the back door," Gentry said. "It's still rainin' a bit."

Paula had recaptured her buoyancy, and her chatter more than made up for the Kid's taciturnity through supper. When he failed to mention the meeting with Chalk she took it on herself to tell Grady. The latter questioned them at length.

"Johnnie had it sized up correctly," he said. "Daggett didn't want to arrest you, Kid; he was trying to scare you out of the country. If you had refused to go he would have jailed you, I suppose, and rigged up something else against you. You were lucky to have Reb show up and take the wind out of his sails with his tale about my having made good on the bronc."

It all seemed so unimportant now to the Kid that he wasn't interested in discussing it. "I've got the money to square my account up with you," he said. "I'll do that this evenin'."

Roberts grinned. "You don't owe me anything, Kid. I never went near Reb Corson about that bronc. He's the man you'll have to square up with."

"What!" the boy jerked out incredulously. "You mean to tell me he made up that story?"

Grady nodded. "Reb can be pretty deep at times."

15

The rain ended before midnight, and morning broke clear and cold. It was the first real threat of winter. The men walked briskly as they went about their work, their breath steaming on the frosty air.

At breakfast the talk was all of the robbery. When Grady came in he was bombarded with questions. "You know as much about it as I do," he told them. "McPartland says something will break in a day or two. I think he's only whistling in the dark. But in the meantime I'm not going to do any wild guessing as to who did the job."

There was work to be done, and he laid it out. The first order of business was to repair all fences while the weather held good. He named the men he wanted to go out with the fencing gang. Stony Justin was to straw-boss the job.

"You'll have to put in new posts, Stony, all along that stretch up above where the fire burned down through the brush. You may find a post or two that's strong enough to stand up against the snow, but there aren't many of them."

Up in the timber to the north, posts had been

cut that summer and piled up to dry. Men had to be assigned to the task of loading and delivering them to the fencing gang. The wire wagon—an ordinary flat-bed wagon fitted out with a platform on which a spool of barbed wire could be placed on a spindle so that it revolved as the team moved along—had to be made ready and men detailed to operate it and keep it supplied. It meant more hauling.

Roberts asked old Homer how the work was coming along on the track.

"Shorty's got two or three days of carpenterin', Grady. I got the harrowin' finished jest right for this rain. As soon as the surface water runs off I'll start draggin' the track. I was goin' to put in for a little new lumber, but under the circumstances I reckon we can pick up enough around the place to finish the job. I don't suppose the boss will feel like spendin' a dollar that can be saved."

"I don't suppose he will," Roberts agreed. "You'll have to knock off for today. Paula wants to go into town this morning. You drive her in and wait around until she has her father ready to bring home."

The men filed out as soon as they had finished eating. The Kid remained at the table, glum and aloof. The problem on his mind was weighing so heavily on him that he could not conceal his preoccupation.

"Haven't you anything to do this morning?" Roberts inquired.

"I can jog the Rocket a little," the Kid replied. "I wouldn't risk takin' him on the road in this mud. You know—those tracks Tuller said he and Daggett followed till they petered out—there must be other damp spots on the way up the crick where they'd show up. I was thinkin' I'd ride up that way this afternoon and have a look."

This was his bid to get away from the ranch so that he could return the money to the cabin.

"Don't bother," said Grady. "The country pitches up too steeply; you'd only be wasting your time." He turned something over in his mind for a moment. "How far up the creek were you yesterday?"

"About half to three quarters of a mile above that old shack." The Kid tried to make it sound casual, wondering where this was leading him.

"What time did you come down?"

"I dunno—late in the afternoon."

"Strange you didn't see anyone, if that's the way our man went. If you had, what a break that would have been for us; we'd have something to work on."

The Kid nodded and did not risk an answer.

The Rocket held little interest for him that morning. At noon he again broached the matter of riding up the creek, more cautiously this time, but again Roberts said no.

Paula brought her father home in the early afternoon. The robbery was as great a mystery as ever. Tuller had learned of the presence of a stranger in the Flat the previous afternoon and was trying to locate him.

The Kid was so beset that he tried to keep out of Grady's way—something he had never expected to find himself doing. He considered stealing away from the ranch that night and going up the creek. But he would need a horse, and that made it impossible. There were too many men around; someone would be sure to see him taking Gyp out of the stable.

It was after ten, and the men had been in bed for an hour before the Kid turned in. Sheer weariness was taking him to sleep, when a thought crossed his mind that jerked him wide awake. What would he do if Daggett went to the cabin and found the money was gone? Chalk wouldn't return a second time.

The inescapable answer made the Kid's head swim. If that happened he'd never be able to pin the robbery on Daggett. Worse still, he'd never be able to clear himself. The money would have to lie where it was forever. In his tortured brain one thought kept repeating itself: he didn't dare to wait any longer; he had to confide in someone.

He couldn't go to Ruxton or Grady and beat around the bush, trying to get their advice; a word to them and he would have to tell all. Saying anything to old Homer, or any of the men, would accomplish nothing. It left only Paula. Could he talk to her? Could he tell her a little without telling all?

She had been quick to suspect him. Maybe she would be just as quick to realize his innocence.

"Paula!" he decided. "I'll tell Paula!"

At breakfast he ate only a mouthful. The course he was to take had seemed clear enough last night. This morning he was of two minds about it. With leaden step he went down to the stables and fed the Rocket and Gyp. In perfunctory fashion he cleaned out the stalls. Old Homer passed and had a cheery word for him. The Kid didn't bother to answer. Instead of brushing the horses he sat down on an overturned bucket, his head between his hands and the corners of his mouth pulled down. He saw Paula coming down the yard, but he continued to sit there, ignoring even Fetch's begging for a caress.

"I shoulda stuck on the wagon with Gran'pap," he muttered disconsolately. "It was the only time in my life I wasn't gettin' into trouble all the while." It was the first time in days that he had thought of old Isaiah.

Paula said good morning and then turned on him inquiringly on seeing that the Rocket hadn't been brushed down. "What's the idea, David? You taking it easy? Suppose you get busy."

"Let it go, Paula," he said without looking up.

"Pull over that box and sit down; I got to talk to you."

"Well?" she queried, not hiding her surprise.

"You remember how you jumped me the other day when you found I had been up the crick, about my gun and everythin'?"

"David, I told you I was so beside myself I didn't know what I was saying," she protested.

"I know. You remember Hoke Tuller sayin' he found tracks leadin' up the crick from the crossin', I reckon. Now Grady says it's funny I didn't see this party on my way down."

"I don't know about that," Paula objected. "The man would have been taking some pains not to be seen."

"But supposin' I did see him," the Kid drove on. "Supposin' I saw him hide somethin'. Supposin' after he left I got a look at it and saw it was a big wad of money—"

"David! Did you?"

"I told you I was just supposin', Paula!" the Kid exclaimed irately. "Can't you use some sense?"

Paula told him she was sorry and begged him to continue.

"Supposin' I had found it—and didn't know nothin' about a robbery—what would you have done if you'd been me? Would you have left the money there for him to come back and get, or would you've taken it and hid it somewheres else till you found out what it was all about?"

"I wouldn't have left it there," Paula said positively. "But I wouldn't have had to wait to find out what it was all about; I'd have known the money was stolen. Men don't hide money that way unless it is stolen." She regarded the Kid with a deeply puzzled air. "Why are you talking this way, David?"

"I'm gettin' to the point," he grumbled. "Supposin' you had hidden the money somewheres and then found you was bein' suspected of the robbery—you'd be in a fix, wouldn't you?"

"Why?"

" 'Cause if you gave the money to the man who was robbed, who would believe your story? If you wanted to put it back where you found it and couldn't do it till after this skunk comes lookin' for it, you'd never be able to say anythin'. He wouldn't keep on comin' back so you could tie anythin' on him."

"He'd only have to come back once if I had anything to do about it," Paula declared. "If I hid some stolen money to keep the thief from making off with it, the first thing I'd do would be to go to the man to whom it belonged and tell him what I'd done."

"How would that clear you?"

"Why, the man wouldn't be such a fool as not to watch the place where the thief hid it. When he showed up to get it he'd be caught. The facts would speak for themselves. How could anyone do anything else but believe me?"

A look of amazement slowly spread over the Kid's face. He could see a way out at last.

"Yeh," he said, "that's right. Catch the thief, and they got to believe me. It's goin' on two days now. Maybe it's too late, but I ain't goin' to waste no more time. Put the money back and watch the place night and day till he shows up! That's it!"

"David!" Paula cried. "Look at me! You haven't been making up this!"

"No, it's true. I got to see your father. I've got the money."

"Oh, David!" Paula hugged him impulsively. Just as suddenly her face sobered. "David—who was it?"

"Chalk Daggett."

Paula waited to hear no more. Taking him by the hand, she started running to the house.

Roberts was in the office with Ruxton when they opened the door.

"Paula, we're busy," said her father. "Do you mind coming back a little later?"

The business he was discussing with Grady was concerned with ways of trimming expenses to make up partially for the loss he had sustained.

"Daddy, this can't wait," she insisted. "Chalk Daggett robbed you. David saw him hide the money."

Ruxton was so startled he couldn't speak for a moment.

"I don't think I'm surprised," Roberts exclaimed. "I thought something was troubling you, Kid. In the name of heaven, why didn't you speak?"

"He was afraid we wouldn't believe him, Grady," said Paula. "It's partly my fault; I started to accuse him."

"Come here, David," Ruxton requested. "Where is the money now?"

"It's safe, Mr. Ruxton; I got it hid under a tree. I saw Daggett ride up to the old cabin on Little Medicine Crick. After he left I went down to see what he'd been doin' there. Fetch got to diggin' in a corner. I thought he was after a mouse. There was a can in the hole, and your money was in it. I didn't know you'd been robbed, but I figured I wasn't goin' to leave it there for Daggett to come back and dig up. I smoothed over the hole and got out of there quick."

Ruxton sighed his relief. "That takes a load off my mind, my boy. I can understand your dilemma. You were like the man who had hold of the bear by the tail and didn't dare to let go."

"He shouldn't have held back," said Grady. "He was after me all day yesterday to let him go up the creek. You could have told me, Kid. I'd have believed you just as much as I believe you now."

"I intended tellin' you, but when I got here that afternoon and heard Mr. Ruxton had been shot—

and what Paula said—I was scared to talk. Gee, I hope you ain't sore at me, Grady."

"I'm not; you can forget that end of it." Roberts turned to Ruxton. "I'm glad it turns out to have been Daggett. I'm glad of it for the Kid's sake as well as my own."

"I know what you mean," said Lee. "He must have been desperate to try it. I don't think there's the slightest chance that we're too late to bait the trap for him."

"Nor I," Roberts agreed. "In fact, we may have a long wait. We'll have to take grub enough with us to last two or three days. And there doesn't want to be any leaks. If a whisper reaches Daggett he won't come within five miles of the cabin."

"No question about that," Ruxton acknowledged. "It means you've got to be careful, Paula. We'll take David with us; that'll leave only you in a position to say anything. A thoughtless word could ruin everything. We'll pull away without telling the men where we're going. When they ask you, say you don't know."

Paula gave him her promise not to say a word. "How soon will you be leaving, Daddy?"

"In a few minutes. I wish you'd go back to the kitchen and have Ling fill a rucksack with grub—stuff that we can eat cold. We won't be able to make a fire. Don't let that Chink know what the grub is for."

Paula left them, and her father unlocked a gun case and selected a rifle. "You take a Thirty-thirty also, Grady. I've got a couple boxes of cartridges."

"I'll take a rifle," Roberts answered, "but if there's a gun fight it'll be at close range . . . I'll catch up the horses. You put your saddle on Gyp, Kid. And you better carry a blanket; it'll be cold up there tonight. When you're ready, ride out of the yard and hit the road as though you were on your way to town. You can haul up after you've got out of sight and wait for us to come along."

He reached for his hat and paused for another word with Ruxton. The Kid was at the door. He backed away from it suddenly. Hoke Tuller was riding up to the house.

"Here comes the sheriff!" he exclaimed. "Tuller!"

"Tuller?" Ruxton echoed, glancing at Roberts, anxious to discover what he made of it. "What do you think, Grady? Shall we say anything to him?"

The tall man hesitated. "I don't know . . . If he'll play it our way I'm for letting him in on it. He can help us."

"He'll have to play it our way!" Ruxton said flatly. "The only chance he has of squaring himself is to get Daggett dead to rights!"

Hoke came in, puffing. He was there to report

that the stranger who had been seen in the Flat had turned out to be an itinerant piano tuner.

"He had a perfect alibi," Tuller informed them. "He was in Judge Hardy's house all afternoon, tinkerin' with the piano. The judge's wife vouched for that. It don't leave us with a thing to go on. I might as well admit it."

"Well, you sit down, Hoke, and listen to me," said Ruxton. "I know who shot me and all the rest of it. When the break comes it's going to be awfully tough on you. The only way you can save your face is to string along with us."

"Who was it, Lee?" the old man demanded grimly.

"Daggett."

"No!"

"I'm telling you, Hoke. I know you've been banged up with your rheumatism and asthma for a couple years and have had to let him do about as he pleased. He's gone hog-wild now. As an old friend, I don't want to throw you overboard. But I'm not excusing you altogether, Hoke."

Tuller pulled out an immense handkerchief and mopped his brow. "I don't blame you," he muttered unhappily. "As you say, I been dependin' on him too much. The dirty skunk! I can see now that he's been cuttin' the ground out from under me almost from the start. I don't know what you want me to do, but I give you my word I'll see it through with you."

Ruxton and Roberts told him the whole story. Their proposed plan to return the money to the hole where Daggett had buried it and then lay out in the brush until he came for it and trap him with the evidence on his person won his approval.

"He'll shore be there lookin' for it," he said. "And he won't wait too long; he'll be afraid of jest what's happened."

"You can make sure he'll show up, Hoke," Roberts told him. "Daggett knows you're out here this morning?"

"Yeh."

"Go back to town. Pick an argument with him—about anything—and then tell him you're going up to Cody for a couple days to see if you can learn anything there; and tell Daggett if he hasn't stirred up something by the time you get back that you're going to ask him to turn in his badge. That'll convince him it's time to run. He'll have you out of the way, and he'll take advantage of it."

Old Hoke nodded his approval. "Sounds all right. I can start for Cody and then cut down through the Slash Hills and be at the cabin by early afternoon."

"Better not ride in," Ruxton advised. "One of us will meet you up the creek a way. That'll be safer."

16

With Hoke hurrying back to town, Roberts and the Kid went down the yard and got up the horses. The latter found a piece of rope that Fetch could not chew so easily and tied up the dog. There was no one in the bunkhouse to question him about taking a blanket. He rolled it and tied it on his saddle. Excitement was running high in him as he rode out of the yard.

With all the furtiveness of an Indian he pulled off the road after he had gone half a mile. No one passed in the ten minutes he waited until Roberts and Ruxton came along.

"Lead the way, David," Ruxton told the Kid.

Keeping well to the east of the creek, the latter led them to the tree where he had left the money. It was there, intact. Without losing any time they proceeded to the cabin and replaced it where Daggett had left it.

Finding cover from which they could keep the old shack under close surveillance was not difficult. Rifles, food, and blankets were carried into the brush. The next step was to conceal the horses.

"Suppose you take them up the creek, Kid,"

said Grady. "Go as far as the end of the fence and picket them somewhere on our side of the line. You can wait around then till Tuller shows up. We'll be hiding out in this patch of junipers. When you come down, work around so you can hit this ravine in back of us. Understand?"

The Kid nodded. "I'll be mighty careful. The two of us been waitin' a long time to square up with that rat. If we don't nail him, it won't be my fault."

He reached the end of the fence in half an hour and found a safe spot for the horses. Returning to the bluff above the creek, he began looking for Hoke. He got through the morning hours without too much impatience; the sheriff had said not to expect him before early afternoon. When the position of the sun told the Kid that it was edging on to two o'clock, his nerves began to snarl. He wasn't too far above the cabin to hear a shot. No sound of gunfire reached him. The feeling was in him, however, that every passing minute brought it nearer.

"I don't want to be stuck up here when they snag that gent!" he grumbled to himself. "We could have handled it without any help from this old butterball Tuller!"

Waiting, his thoughts winged back inevitably to that spring morning when he had waited with Elmer above the Stinking Water. Between then and now the wheel of life had described an almost complete circle. He wasn't running from Daggett today; it was the other way around: it was Chalk who was being stalked.

The Kid had never wavered in his determination to bring Daggett to account for killing Elmer, but just what that meant, or how it was to be accomplished, had always remained an obscure and nebulous matter in his mind. Despite all his vagueness, he had carried the thought that Chalk must die. Sending him off to prison for a long term of years had never occurred to the Kid.

It posed a question, and he thought it out carefully. Daggett's death was desirable, but he didn't insist on it. "If he gets fifteen years I'll be satisfied," he told himself. "That'll bust him; he'll never be able to come back."

When he finally saw Tuller coming he remained hidden until the old man was almost on top of him before he popped out. It gave Hoke a start, and he reached for his gun.

"That was a dang-fool trick!" he growled. "I might have blown yore head off! Did I get here in time?"

"I ain't heard no shootin'," the Kid answered. "You're to leave your horse here. I got the others back in the trees."

With the Kid leading the way, they reached the ravine in back of Roberts and Ruxton. When they emerged from it they saw Grady beckoning to them.

"No sign of him yet, eh?" Hoke queried.

"Not yet. The two of you crawl in here with us. We were just having a bite to eat."

The Kid was hungry and he helped himself to a slice of meat and a biscuit. The three men discussed exactly what they would do when Daggett appeared. They agreed they would let him enter the cabin, get the money, and then the sheriff was to call on him to surrender as he reached the door.

"If he throws up his hands, all right," said Hoke. "If he goes for his gun, shoot him down."

Their vigil went for naught that afternoon. Several reasons why Daggett might think it safer to come by night suggested themselves. Midnight passed without bringing him. There was a chill in the air that ate into Tuller's bones. Ruxton told him to curl up in a blanket and try to catch a little sleep; that he would stand guard for a couple of hours, with Roberts taking over from then to daylight.

The Kid tried to keep awake, but he kept dozing off, and when he fell asleep about two he didn't open his eyes until the sun was streaming down into the creek bottoms.

"You didn't miss anything," Grady told him, reading his thought. "The only visitor we had was that big coyote you took the shot at."

As the morning wore on and their watching proved fruitless, Ruxton's confidence began to wane. "He must have smelled a mouse, Hoke. Are you sure you didn't tip him off by accident?"

"Absolutely! If somethin's gone haywire, you'll have to look somewheres else for it." He studied the Kid for several minutes. "Lee," he inquired soberly, "what makes you and Roberts so sure the boy is tellin' a straight story?"

"He took us to the money," Ruxton answered, bristling. "That ought to be proof enough for you. Let's not get to wrangling about that."

Noon passed, and still there was no sign of Chalk. Capturing Daggett had seemed such a sure and simple matter that the Kid had entertained no serious doubt as to the outcome. Now he was torn with misgiving, all his feeling of certainty gone.

"Ruxton can say what he pleases," was his brooding thought, "but if Daggett never shows up, he'll always have the feelin' that I robbed him and then lost my nerve and gave the money back. Reckon Grady'll think the same."

The thought was dashed from his mind a moment later, when Roberts jerked out a low, warning cry. The Kid looked down the creek, and there was Daggett, riding along on his piebald bronc, casting glances left and right as though to make sure he had the bottoms to himself.

The Kid could hear his heart pounding. Roberts flicked a warning glance at him.

Chalk slid from the saddle and after another suspicious glance hurried into the cabin. They could hear him digging. Tuller raised up on his knees and drew his gun. As Grady had said, the range was short; a rifle wasn't necessary.

Suddenly Daggett was at the door.

"Reach!" Hoke roared. "We got you covered!"

He should have waited another second, got his man out in the open. But it was too late for that now. Daggett spun around on his heels and sprang back into the cabin. He didn't linger there. Running across the room, he crawled through the window on the far side and waited, gun in hand, for a target.

"Look out for him!" Roberts cried. "He'll shoot through the window! Hoke, you and the boss go around in front; I'll work around in back!"

"You're throwin' your life away, Chalk!" Tuller called. "Give up or we'll kill you!"

Daggett answered with a blast of gunfire. The Kid, ordered to lay stretched out in the junipers, heard a slug whine over his head.

Chalk got a flash of Tuller as he leaped past the door. He fired instantly, the slug splintering the jamb and driving a sliver into the sheriff's cheek.

"Don't try to take the rat alive!" Hoke yelled. "Kill him!"

Daggett realized his position was desperate. He might be able to hold them off for a few minutes, but that wouldn't win the day for him; he had to reach his bronc. He glanced at the rear corner of the cabin and saw Roberts's gun leveling at him.

He snapped a shot at it and then leaped back to the brush and started running to his horse.

With a hand that had grown less steady with the years, Hoke threw down on him and squeezed the trigger. Grady fired at almost the same instant, the two shots so closely spaced they sounded as one. Daggett's momentum carried him another step before he fell in a diving crash. Either one of the shots would have killed him.

The Kid scrambled to his feet and ran past Ruxton. Hoke was turning Chalk over with his boot. The old man's face was smeared with blood from the deeply embedded sliver.

"He had his chance," Tuller said.

"More than he was in the habit of giving other men," Grady added. "You better take charge of your money, Mr. Ruxton."

The Kid walked away, feeling a little nauseated. Chalk was not a pretty sight. His death meant that Elmer's account had been settled in full. But, strangely, it wasn't Elmer who engaged the boy's thoughts. It was Paula. She had questioned him, but she had had faith in him too. She would know now that her faith hadn't been misplaced. It was as though he had moved out from under a shadow—not only the shadow of the past several days but one under which he had been living for months.

Grady came over to where he stood and put an arm around him. "This closes the book on some things for us, Kid," he said with deep feeling. "If you'll take my advice, you'll keep it closed and get it out of your mind. Forget all the killing you've seen these past months. I'd even forget Elmer. You've got better days ahead of you. I don't know what you want to make of yourself, but you rate a chance, and you're going to get it . . . You better bring down the horses. You can get back to the house then. Paula's undoubtedly worrying herself sick over us."

In the days that followed, the Kid would have been surprised had he known how often he was the subject of Ruxton's conversations with Grady. The two of them came down to the track and watched the workouts. Their interest in the way Paula and the Kid were bringing the Rocket along only partly explained their presence.

"David's going to take him around once more," Paula called to her father one morning. "You hold the watch on him, Daddy."

Jogging down the track with the Kid, she said, "Let's give them a thrill, David. I'll stay with you as long as I can, and you keep the Rocket moving. I know you can bring him in under thirty-six seconds."

She was deliriously happy these days, and the Kid found her gaiety contagious. "Okay!" he said with a grin. "I'll have you eatin' dust before I hit the stretch."

Grady started them. Before they were around the first turn he knew what they were up to. "They're going to show us something this time, boss," he called to Ruxton. "Look at him! He's really letting the Rocket out!"

Gyp couldn't hold the pace and began to drop back before they rounded the far turn. The Kid had been aching for this opportunity to find out what the Rocket could really do, and he drove down the stretch as though his life depended on it.

After he flashed under the wire he went around the track, and by the time he jogged up to the stand Paula had the good news.

"Daddy clocked you in thirty-five and a quarter, David!" she cried excitedly. "The record for three furlongs is only thirty-three!"

"It certainly looks as though we had a horse this time," Ruxton declared happily. "If you youngsters keep this up, we'll go further than Cody next fall . . . By the way, David, I want you to come up to the house this evening for dinner. Grady's coming over too. I've got a little surprise for you."

The Kid thought Paula looked as though she knew what the surprise was, and he tried his best to pry the secret out of her as they walked the horses.

"I don't know a thing about it," she insisted, her airy manner further convincing him that she did.

"I just hope he ain't goin' to offer me a reward for findin' his money," the Kid said crossly. "I wouldn't take it!"

"I guess Dad realizes that," Paula replied.

"It can't be anythin' about that bronc of Reb Corson's. I tried to pay him, and he wouldn't take a dime." The Kid's head went up as an idea flashed across his mind, and he gazed at Paula with something akin to terror. "Paula—he ain't thinkin' of makin' me go to school! He can't do that to me!"

"Don't worry, he won't," she said with a laugh. "But I'm going to do something about it this winter. I've got a lot of books. You don't want to be just a cowpuncher, do you?"

"Well, I don't know as I do," the Kid answered uneasily.

"Then you have to have an education."

The Kid shook his head, enormously sober. "I dunno," he said.

"What do you mean, you don't know?" she demanded, jumping down from her perch on the half door of the Rocket's stall. Her tone was both anxious and annoyed. "That's part of the surprise, David! Daddy and Grady are going to Chicago in the early spring to a big Hereford Association show. If you buckle down this winter with the books, Dad says he'll take us along with him . . . Well, aren't you surprised—and excited about it?" she asked with rising indignation as the Kid's face reflected no sign of enthusiasm.

"He don't owe me no trip to Chicago," he said, pulling down a dry blanket and opening the stall door.

"Course he doesn't, silly! You've got to earn the trip. You don't get a chance to go to Chicago every day, David . . . Don't you want to go?"

"I sure do—if I can earn the trip." The Kid's eyes brightened suddenly and his thin face began to glow with eagerness. "That'd sure be fine—goin' to Chicago!" He knew he had her to thank, but embarrassment gripped him when he tried to express his gratitude.

He couldn't understand it, but in some vague way Paula had begun to hold a new interest for him. For the first time he felt shy and self-conscious in her presence.

"I reckon we wouldn't have to be lookin' at Herefords all the time," he said. "When I get to Chicago I want to see that Two Bills Show Shorty is always talkin' about. They've got a big cowboy band that comes out on horseback, and there's a singer comes out with them, all dressed in white buckskin—"

Paula nodded; she had heard Shorty's tales.

"Shorty says they pay him a hundred dollars a night just for singin'," the Kid continued, a faraway look in his eyes.

"Shorty's an awful liar, David!" Paula declared with unexplained vehemence. She had read the

Kid's thought and was suddenly afraid. "You better come down to earth."

"What do you mean?"

"David—are you thinking of going back with that old fake on the medicine wagon?"

Paula's heart was in her eyes. It dried the Kid's throat to look at her.

"No, I couldn't do that," he managed, looking away. "I'd miss Grady too much—and your father—and—and you."

Paula smiled at him fondly. "Gee, it's sweet of you to say that, David!"

Without warning she caught his face in her hands and kissed his cheek. Before the Kid could throw off the spell of it she was running up the yard, her laughter trailing after her.

"No question about it," the Kid murmured with a heavy sigh, "this is where I belong!"